"Will I get an eviction notice if I kiss you once?" Bain asked.

"Once?" Erin whispered.

Her trembling mouth looked lush and red, simply begging to be taken. He leaned in closer and traced the lushness with his finger. "Make it twice."

Erin sighed against the sweetness of his kiss, and every doubt she'd harbored about Bain disintegrated into a pool of desire. Her arms encircled his neck and brought them into closer contact. This was the kiss she'd dreamed of all the night before.

Bain felt every nerve ending in his body snap to life as she moved against him. He wanted Erin with an intensity that shocked him. In a flash he had Erin pressed against the kitchen wall, devouring her with feverish kisses. And the more he demanded, the more sweetly she surrendered. . . .

WHAT ARE *LOVESWEPT* ROMANCES?

They are stories of true romance and touching emotion. We believe those two very important ingredients are constants in our highly sensual and very believable stories in the LOVESWEPT line. Our goal is to give you, the reader, stories of consistently high quality that may sometimes make you laugh, sometimes make you cry, but are always fresh and creative and contain many delightful surprises within their pages.

Most romance fans read an enormous number of books. Those they truly love, they keep. Others may be traded with friends and soon forgotten. We hope that each LOVESWEPT romance will be a treasure—a "keeper." We will always try to publish

LOVE STORIES YOU'LL NEVER FORGET BY AUTHORS YOU'LL ALWAYS REMEMBER

The Editors

Loveswept® 629

IN
DADDY'S ARMS

MARCIA
EVANICK

BANTAM BOOKS
NEW YORK · TORONTO · LONDON · SYDNEY · AUCKLAND

IN DADDY'S ARMS

A Bantam Book / July 1993

If you would be interested in receiving protective vinyl covers for your
Loveswept books, please write to this address for information:

Loveswept
Bantam Books
P.O. Box 985
Hicksville, NY 11802

ISBN 0-553-44327-5

Published simultaneously in the United States and Canada

Bantam Books are published by Bantam Books, a division of Bantam Doubleday Dell Publishing Group, Inc. Its trademark, consisting of the words
"Bantam Books" and the portrayal of a rooster, is Registered in U.S. Patent
and Trademark Office and in other countries. Marca Registrada. Bantam
Books, 1540 Broadway, New York, New York 10036.

PRINTED IN THE UNITED STATES OF AMERICA

OPM   0 9 8 7 6 5 4 3 2 1

To Beth.
This one is for you.

PROLOGUE

Bain O'Neil stared out at the dismal view beyond the rain-streaked window. All he could see were huge office buildings, apartment buildings, brick monstrosities, and dreary rain. Dark, heavy clouds hung above the city, or was it a fat layer of pollution being forced back down for his viewing pleasure? In New York it was hard to tell. March in the Big Apple was the pits. It wasn't cold enough for drifts of freshly fallen snow to cover the grime, and spring wouldn't dare show itself yet, if only because he had been watching for it for weeks. Spring was the sign of hope. Spring brought color into the city, into his world. He was waiting for spring and the results of a test that would affect the rest of his life.

Bain shifted uncomfortably in the hospital bed and muttered a curse. He'd be damned if he would be caught lying in bed like some invalid when old Doc

O'Donnell finally made his appearance and delivered the long-awaited news.

With a few groans Bain slowly and painfully made his way to the huge imitation leather chair, with its saggy bottom and hard springs, that sat in front of the window. For the hundredth time he cursed the men who had done this to him, Julio, José, and the Sanchez brothers. Life in prison was too good for those scum. They each deserved a cellmate who was six foot seven, two hundred and forty pounds of raw power, and hated dark-eyed Latin men.

He lowered himself into the chair and propped his battered and torn leg against the metal siderailing of his bed. With great care he closed the front of his robe over the bandages. He hated the gold-color robe his mother had brought him. He hated the stack of brand-new pajamas his brothers had given him, and he hated the fluffy brown slippers his sister had so tearfully presented to him during a visit. Over ten years of doing undercover work on the best police force in America, and he ended up sitting in some dingy hospital room looking like Winnie-the-Pooh.

Bain had always known that undercover work was one of the toughest jobs in the NYPD, but he had never realized how tough until three weeks earlier when his cover had been blown. Julio, José, and the ever-charming Sanchez brothers had taken great pleasure in trying to work, or more accurately to cut, information out of Bain before they would totally eliminate him. Bain had figured he was a dead man either way, so he'd kept his mouth shut and used every ounce of strength to fight the pain the deadly switchblade was inflicting. They had started slicing three inches away from his most precious organ, carving flesh and muscle into ribbons. When a six-man backup team finally broke down the warehouse door and saved Bain, he had been a mere quarter inch away from becoming a soprano for life.

A shudder shook his body as Bain remembered every detail of that night. His hands tightened on the arms of the chair, and he glared at the filthy window. The soft opening and closing of a door told him the waiting was finally over. Dr. O'Donnell had arrived.

"Oh, good, you're up."

Bain slowly turned his head to look at Shamus O'Donnell. This was the doctor who had delivered him and his four siblings. This was the doctor who had sewn up his arm when he fell off his bike and needed sixteen stitches. This was the doctor who had insisted on assisting in the operating room while a team of surgeons worked miracles to save Bain's life and leg. This was the same doctor who had stayed by his side in intensive care day and night until he was out of danger. For the first time Bain could remember, Dr. Shamus O'Donnell looked unnerved. Bain's heart sank. "Well?"

Dr. O'Donnell glanced at the clipboard clutched in his hand and roughly cleared his throat. "The good news is that you will be able to perform normally while having relationships."

Bain raised an eyebrow. "I figured that one out for myself when I gave you the sample." His glance fell to the clipboard. "What are the results?"

The doctor slowly sat down on the edge of the unmade bed. "I'm sorry, Bain. The initial test shows you're sterile."

Bain turned away as tears filled his eyes. He would never be a father! He would never hold a wailing newborn in his arms and know it was his. His worst nightmare was coming true. When he had awakened in intensive care, he hadn't asked if he would ever walk again. His first question had been if he'd be able to father children. Now he knew the answer. He watched as drops of rain splattered against the window, tuning out Dr. O'Donnell, who was saying something about time and performing a second test after his rehabilitation and therapy were completed.

Spring wasn't coming. All the colors in Bain's life had been washed away by a cold March rain and four furious drug dealers. The team of surgeons should have saved their time and let him die. A tear slid down his cheek as the doctor's mumbling droned on behind him. Bain's hands gripped the chair harder as the tears came faster. He would never have a family of his own.

ONE

Bain O'Neil pulled his car over to the side of the road and stared at the brightly painted mailbox. The yellow paint outshone the sun, and deep-purple letters proudly proclaimed that the Flynns resided at 56 Wild Flower Road. Someone had also taken the time to paint miniature pink and purple flowers across the side of the box. He glanced to the right, but could only detect the slightest outline of a house through the thick trees. If he finally wanted to put his mind at ease and get on with the rest of his life, he would have to drive up the gravel lane and face his obsession for the last three months.

He raised his dark sunglasses and rubbed at his tired eyes. Streaks of moisture dampened his hand. Did the Finger Lakes district of New York have to be so breathtaking in the summertime? Did the damn mailbox have to be so cheerful? He had already accepted what he couldn't have in life, but the merry little box seemed to mock him anew. Bain O'Neil was never to know the happiness and love of his very own family. When Dr. O'Donnell had entered his hospital room and told him the results of the test, all of Bain's hopes and dreams had been sucked away into a gray vacuum. The word *sterile* had screamed off the pale hospital walls and echoed down the long, dark tunnel that had held his future.

In the three months that followed, Bain had pushed himself unmercifully through rehabilitation with one goal in mind: He wanted a glimpse of the two children he had helped father. The term "sperm donor" left an ugly taste in his mouth, but that was what he had been, not once, but twice.

He had always looked on it as repaying a favor to Doc O'Donnell, who had saved his father's life twenty-five years earlier when his father had been shot in the chest. Over five years ago the doctor had asked Bain if he would consider making a "donation" for some unfortunate Irish couple from Brooklyn who couldn't complete the job without a little help. Bain had known he had been asked because he was young, healthy, and Irish. Doc knew his family background and could guarantee the couple a healthy, normal father. He had gladly done "the deed." Two years later the doctor had asked for another "donation" for the same couple. They had wanted a second child and preferred to use the same donor.

Four months earlier Bain's male pride and ego wouldn't have fit in the same car with him. He had been wonder cop, awesome brother and uncle, and superstud. Hell, he could impregnate ladies without being in the same city. Bain lowered his sunglasses. It was amazing what a few scum-of-the-earth individuals could do to a man.

He shifted the car back into drive and glanced down at the local newspaper lying on the passenger seat. It was folded to the "For Sale" section. Circled in red ink was an advertisement for an antique pie safe at 156 Lakeshore Drive. He was willing to play the stupid tourist who couldn't read a road sign, let alone a house number. After seeing the children, he was hopping back into the car and heading west. He wasn't going to take his foot off the gas pedal until he reached his destination in North Dakota. He hadn't come to the Flynns to cause trouble or to announce who he was, he just wanted to go to his grave with the image of what his children would have looked like.

Sweat moistened his palms as he steered the car onto the gravel drive. He placed a fist against his chest and groaned at the heavy thumping of his heart. In a matter of minutes, when he drove away, he wouldn't even have its companionship. Bain already knew he was going to be leaving his heart behind.

Envy filled his soul as he rounded a curve and the house came into view. It stood two and a half stories high and was pale yellow and white. Bain figured it was at least a hundred years old, if not older. Flowers in every conceivable color overflowed window boxes, huge pots sitting on the porch, and gardens that wrapped the house in a kaleidoscope of color. Massive trees dotted the yard, inviting a person to sit in their shade and relax. Cayuga Lake, the second largest of the several Finger Lakes, bordered the property. A huge, two-story boathouse stood majestically on its shore. Bain felt like crying.

He parked next to a plain white van, grabbed up the newspaper, and before he lost his nerve, got out of the car. He was three steps away from the front porch when the sound of children's laughter captured his attention. In a daze he walked around to the back of the house, past six plastic-and-glass greenhouses in desperate need of repair, and toward the high-pitched squeals of delight.

As he turned the corner of the house, his feet faulted and without the support of his cane he would have lost his balance. Fresh morning dew coated his sneakers and the tip of his cane as he watched a young woman hang laundry and two little girls play with a black-and-gray-striped kitten. He had two daughters!

Laughter faded away into silence as the girls and woman noticed him standing there. Bain forced his gaze away from the girls as the woman finished pinning a tiny pair of pink shorts to the line and walked toward him.

"Hello, may I help you?"

Bain swallowed hard. The woman's voice was one-quarter Irish brogue, one-quarter Brooklyn accent, and all angel. A gentle summer breeze teased the ends of her waist-length hair. It was the color of a blazing sunset and looked twice as soft as heaven. Laughing green eyes gazed up at him, and Bain swallowed the lump in his throat. This was the mother of his children? Life was not only unfair, it was cruel. If the two little girls peering around their mother's skirt hadn't already stolen his heart, Bain would have sworn Cupid's misdirected arrow had just pierced it.

"Are you all right, sir?" The woman shifted her gaze from his face to his cane.

Bain forced himself out of his stupor. He raised the newspaper being crushed in his fist and tried to remember what exactly he was supposed to be inquiring about. "I'm here about the ad you placed."

"Oh, good! I was beginning to worry that no one would ever respond."

Bain frowned. "Excuse me?"

The woman wiped her damp hands on her skirt and shook his hand. "I know the ad has only been running for three weeks, but you're the first one to come."

He dropped her hand as desire snapped at his fingertips. This was another man's wife, not the recipient of his seed—a sterile vial had served in that purpose. "I am?"

"I'm sure you're anxious to see the apartment." She turned toward the boathouse and grabbed hold of each child's hand. "Oh, by the way, I'm Erin Flynn, and these are my daughters—Caitlin"—she raised the older girl's hand—"and Arlene." Dropping Arlene's hand, she pushed a lock of red hair out of the two-year-old's eyes and tried to erase a streak of mud from the child's cheek.

Bain slowly followed her as she walked toward the boathouse. His leg throbbed, his head pounded, and the hole in his chest, where his heart had once beat, ached. What he needed was a massive dose of reality and to get out of there fast. He didn't want to see any apartment. He didn't want the delectable sway of this fiery-haired angel's hips within his sight. He glanced at Caitlin as she smiled over her shoulder at him, then closed his eyes in anguish. Caitlin was the spitting image of his sister, Autumn.

He cleared his throat. "Maybe I should wait until

your husband comes home so we can discuss the arrangements?" He knew he could make it past Niagara Falls, through Ontario, and into Michigan before Cameron Flynn arrived home for dinner.

Erin stopped and turned. Did she seem incapable of handling something so simple as renting out an apartment? Desperation started to claw at her gut. For the past two years she had been cutting more corners than a doughnut maker. She needed a tenant in the apartment. Sensing her turbulent emotions, her daughters buried themselves deeper into her long cotton skirt. "I'm sorry, Mister . . . ?"

"O'Neil. Bain O'Neil."

"Well, then, Mr. O'Neil, all business arrangements must be through me. My husband passed away two years ago." She wasn't afraid to admit she and the girls were alone. Bain O'Neil didn't strike her as criminal, and her intuition had never failed her yet. She glanced quickly at his cane. Actually Bain reminded her of a wounded animal looking for a place to heal. As long as he could pay the rent on the apartment, she'd be more than grateful to allow him to recuperate there. She needed the additional income to expand her business and repair the greenhouses so she could support herself and the girls. Cameron's insurance money was dwindling faster than she could say the name of the dreaded disease that had taken his life a short eight weeks after being diagnosed.

Bain felt his jaw drop open. Erin was a widow! He glanced at the two bright-eyed girls who didn't have a father. Hell, that wasn't right. They did have a father, and he was standing right in front of them. What they didn't have was a daddy. Bain wanted to be that daddy more than anything else in the world. "I'm sorry, Mrs. Flynn. I didn't know."

"Thank you, and please call me Erin. Would you like to see the apartment now?"

It was on the tip of his tongue to say he'd take it sight unseen, but he knew better. Erin would think something was fishy if he did. "Yes, please." There was no way he was leaving there and allowing her to raise his daughters on her own. God had granted him a reprieve. He might not have been there for their conceptions or births, but it would take the devil himself to remove him from their lives now. He followed Erin over to the boathouse and frowned at the wooden stairs leading to the second floor. They didn't look too steady.

Caitlin was already halfway up the steps, and before he could stop her, Erin picked up Arlene and climbed the stairs. Bain held his breath as the stairs creaked and groaned under their weight. At the top landing Erin pushed open the door and allowed her children to enter the apartment. She looked down the steps and frowned. "Aren't you coming, Mr. O'Neil?" When he hobbled up onto the first step with the use of his cane, she cried in dismay, "Your leg!"

Bain maneuvered up the steps without hesitation. The pain throbbing in his leg wasn't nearly as bad as it once had been. Every day he was improving. "I'm fine. Don't worry."

Erin bit her lower lip as she watched him make his way up the stairs. When he reached the landing and deck area, she hurried inside and scowled at the girls, who were bouncing on the couch. "Stop that," she whispered.

Bain ducked his head to hide his grin. Caitlin and Arlene definitely had O'Neil blood flowing through their veins. He would bet his entire disability income that Erin had cursed the unknown sperm donor more than once. For the first time he examined their clothes instead of their angelic faces. Caitlin's were smeared with grass stains and dirt, apparently from her rolling around in the yard with the kitten. Arlene not only looked like she had spent the morning making mud pies, but the dirt smeared across her face showed she had been tasting them too.

Their disheveled appearance caused him to smile. His girls were beautiful, active, and lovingly normal. How was it possible for them to steal his heart again? His smile slipped as he glanced at their mother.

Erin seemed nervous and edgy. As Bain's mother loved to say, any woman raising an O'Neil was a woman living on the edge. The edge of what was never clarified, but Erin Flynn looked to be straddling one. Did his presence here alarm her? Or was he spending too much time watching the girls? Lord, maybe she thought he was some type of pervert. After ten years of working for the New York City Police Department, he had seen every kind of pervert slither out from underneath some strange rocks. Erin had every right to be cautious. Hell, they were his kids she was protecting.

He glanced around the apartment with little interest, since he was taking it no matter what. He didn't like the idea that his daughters were living outside of a town with the nearest neighbor a quarter of a mile away. The dull, serviceable kitchen blended into an equally dull living room that obviously had to double as the bedroom. A miniature closet and bathroom were tucked away in the corner. On the back wall what had to be the first sliding glass doors ever installed revealed a stunning view of the lake.

"Well, Mr. O'Neil," Erin said after a couple minutes of silence, "as you can see, it comes completely furnished. You'll have everything you need, except for your linens of course."

Bain turned from the remarkable view of the lake

and kept his gaze away from the girls. "What are you asking a month?"

Erin frowned. "It was in the ad."

He had been afraid of that. "I mean, what are you really asking?"

"I'm afraid, Mr. O'Neil, that I have to stick to the original price."

She named a monthly fee that caused Bain to gasp. Was she serious? How could anyone rent an apartment at such a ridiculously low rate? He glanced around the large room again. There were no gaping holes in the roof, and the floor appeared solid. Doors, windows, and the four walls looked like they could hold out the elements. So where was the catch? "The utilities are extra?"

She closed her eyes briefly, then said, "Yes."

In that moment Bain realized how afraid she was that he wasn't going to take the apartment. He could detect the stubborn pride that kept her back straight, the steely determination in the slight tilt of her jaw. Erin Flynn was a sight to behold when she was holding her ground. He couldn't have picked a better woman to raise his children. "I'm sorry if I seemed shocked by such a low price. In New York City, if you are lucky enough to find one, an apartment can cost you three times as much, plus your first-born child."

Erin chuckled. "Tell me something I don't know."

Bain slid a quick glance at the miniature red-haired angels opening the kitchen cabinets and curiously peeking inside. "The price seems more than fair, Erin," he said, looking back at her. "Will you be wanting two months' security along with the first month's rent?"

He could almost see the relief washing through her. "That would be fine, Mr. O'Neil."

"Since we're going to be neighbors, why don't you call me Bain." He frowned. Everything was going too easily. Didn't she know anything about being a landlord? "Don't you want to see my references first?" He had had the list typed out when he'd left New York on his way to a small town in North Dakota, where an assistant-deputy job was waiting for him. He would have to call and let them know he was now turning down the job. Nothing was more important than his girls.

"References," Erin repeated, a blush sweeping up her cheeks. "Yes, of course."

"I have them and my checkbook in the car."

"What about your leg?"

Bain glanced down at it. "What about it?"

"I don't mean to be nosy, but will you be okay with a second-floor apartment?"

He held up the cane. "In a couple of weeks I won't be needing this any longer. Climbing those steps a few times a day will be perfect therapy."

She smiled. "Really?"

"Really." He stared at her, thinking that her smile not only lit up her face and the room, it brought the first signs of colors whirling back into his life. The fates had been with him last month when he had broken into Doc O'Donnell's office and gone through his files. It had taken him three hours of searching through every patient's file until he'd hit upon the right one. He was eternally thankful that Erin's last name was Flynn instead of Zuckerman. He knew what he had done was not only criminally wrong, but it was morally wrong, too, but he'd do it again tomorrow just to see her smile.

A loud crashing sound filled the apartment. Both Erin and Bain quickly turned and spotted Arlene standing innocently in the middle of a pile of mismatched pots and pans. Bain chuckled while Erin rushed over and started to put the cookware back into the cabinet. "Arlene Corey Flynn, surely the saints had to be on vacation the day you were born."

Arlene raised her mischievous gaze to Bain and beamed.

Bain's chuckle turned into a full-fledged laugh. His parents, brothers, and sister would have given anything to have accomplished what this sparkling-eyed imp had done in twenty minutes. Arlene Corey Flynn had given him back the joy of laughter.

Erin lovingly frowned at her younger daughter

as she jammed two lids back into the cabinet and shut the door. "That was bad, young lady."

Arlene's angelic smile shone through the dirt on her face as she raised her arms. "Mommy, up, please."

Erin hoisted the child up and glared at Bain, who was still laughing. "I would appreciate it, Bain, if you didn't encourage her."

Bain innocently raised his hands. "All I did was laugh."

"That's all the encouragement she needs. Arlene here is an actress. She loves playing for an audience."

He tried to look stern at the cherub resting her head against Erin's shoulder, but couldn't. Who could possibly be upset with the most beautiful child in the world? He glanced at Caitlin, who was standing back enjoying the show. Correction, he thought. Make that one of the two most beautiful children in the world.

Erin looked at Bain and groaned. He had obviously fallen under the spell her two daughters always managed to cast on any male within their reach. Total domination. She could well understand her daughters' fascination with Bain, though. He was gorgeous. With a name like Bain O'Neil he had to be as Irish as Saint Paddy's Day. Erin had developed a weakness for big, strong Irish lads in the seventh grade, when Donovan O'Hare saved her from the evil clutches of Bradley Smith, who was demanding a kiss. She had followed that weakness all through high school and into college. Tightening her grip on Arlene, Erin pulled herself back to the present. Bain wasn't auditioning for the role of lover, he was going to be her tenant.

"Will Mrs. O'Neil like to look at the apartment before you write out the check?" she asked, congratulating herself on not coming directly out and asking him if he was married.

"The last place my mother inspected was my dorm room, and she vowed to keep her opinions to herself from that day forward."

"You're not married?"

"No."

"Children?"

He stiffened slightly and paled. His answer was slow in coming. "No."

Erin tilted her head and studied his guarded expression. Was he hiding something? "What kind of work do you do?" She was finally getting into her role as landlord. Under this disguise she could find out everything she wanted to know about him.

"I'm an ex-police officer."

"Ex?" Her gaze slid down to his leg and cane.

"I'm collecting full disability now, but once the leg heals completely, I could resume my career in a limited capacity."

She picked up on the mysterious undercurrents in his voice. "Oh, I'm sorry."

"Don't be. I finally have the time to sit down and do something I've always wanted to do."

"What's that?"

"Write." At her startled look he explained, "Didn't you know that most police officers are frustrated writers?"

"No." She smiled and smoothed her fingers over Arlene's soft hair. It looked like naptime was approaching faster than normal this morning. "What kind of book are you writing? Wait, don't tell me, let me guess. A detective mystery."

Bain followed the rhythmic motion of her hand and watched as Arlene's eyes drifted shut. The first hundred pages of his manuscript were sitting in a box in the backseat of his car. It was more than the average whodunit. It was dark, lethal, and full of reality. It portrayed a world filled with scum, where murderers walked away on technicalities and the good guys never finished first. It showed corrupt judges, cops on the take, and the innocent citizens of the city becoming victims of the system as well as of the crime. Bain hated those first one hundred pages, but the department's psychologist had told him to keep writing. It was therapy.

"Right," he answered Erin. "It's a story about two homicide cops." He didn't mention that it took place in the cesspool of the city. Anyone reading the first five pages would undoubtedly get the picture. He'd described it in great detail.

"Well, good luck with it."

"Thanks." He noticed her shift Arlene's weight. "Isn't she getting heavy?"

"Believe me, it's easier to carry them now than it was before they were born."

He glanced down at her flat stomach and tried to picture her when she'd carried his child. She had probably glowed and was full of energy as she toted around her precious cargo. Just like his sister and sisters-in-law. "You seemed to have made it through admirably."

She smiled at some distant memory. "*Admirably* isn't quite the word I would use, but thanks." She winked at Caitlin and smiled down at the top of Arlene's head. "How about I go lay this one down for her nap? When you're done looking the place over, stop by the house and you can give me the references and your check. When do you want to move in?"

"Today."

"Today?"

"That isn't a problem, is it?"

"No," she said quickly. "Not at all."

Erin leaned against the window frame and stared out into the night. Pale light spilled out of the boathouse apartment, lighting the deck and the top of the wooden steps. She could barely see the outline of Bain sitting in the darkness on a folding chair, his feet propped up on the railing. Something about him disturbed her and she couldn't put her finger on it. She could understand the physical attraction. Heck, she was only human, after all. He was sweet and gentle with the girls. He had bought a box of ice-cream pops when he'd gone into town that afternoon to pick up some things he needed. He had ceremoniously given each girl one after all his groceries had been unloaded and carried upstairs. Actually Erin had carried most of the bags, but it had been worth it just to see the grins on her daughters' faces as they bit into their frozen treats.

Erin would hate to admit it, but she had called every one of his references. She had received nothing but glowing reports. His former landlord swore he was the best tenant ever, and even his lieutenant from the force seemed to take it hard that Bain had moved out of the city. He seemed to be the perfect tenant, just what she had been looking for. So why this unease? Why did she feel his presence there was going to change her life? And why did she have this awful feeling that Bain was hiding something?

TWO

Bain breathed a sigh of relief as Erin disappeared from the window and the curtain fell back into place. He had known the moment she had left her bed to stand at the window. Policeman's intuition was a hell of a thing. His old lieutenant used to say he had eyes like a cat, senses like a wolf, and followed more hunches than Columbo. The lieutenant was wrong. Bain was an O'Neil, born and bred to become one of NYPD's finest. It was in the blood.

Only one O'Neil had left the NYPD before him—Autumn. His sister had the heart of an angel and the soul of an artist. She didn't belong in the streets fighting the bad guys. His father and he had secretly celebrated the day Autumn turned in her badge. When his father had suggested that Bain might also be suited for something else in life, Bain had blamed the nutty idea on the few *cold ones* his father had knocked back. Incredibly he had asked his father, "Like what?" His father's response—"A writer"—had floored him. How had his father known about his secret childhood wish? He had laughed it off and proudly explained that O'Neil men were policemen, just like the Kennedys were Democrats. They were inseparable. Rory O'Neil had said the world would still go round if one of the Kennedys switched parties, and Bain had quickly changed the subject. Some dreams were never meant to be.

Who would have thought that four years after that conversation with his father his words would come true? If there was one thing in life that irritated Bain, it was boredom. He craved adventure. That was why he'd always relished the most dangerous undercover assignments. That was why he'd been one of the best.

He couldn't live the adventures any longer, but he could write about them. The department's psychologist had been right in suggesting he follow his childhood dream for a while. Writing was therapeutic. Every day he poured out his frustrations, filling page after page with bitter resentment.

Bain shuddered at the black memories and forced his gaze back onto the house not forty yards away. Amazingly the memories that had plagued his every waking hour and haunted his dreams slipped farther away. Arlene's mischievous smile had returned laughter to his life, and Caitlin's sweet innocence gave him back the gift of hope. What would Erin show him?

He cautiously lowered his right leg from the railing. The muscles in his inner thigh were screaming for relief. He started to massage the cramped muscles as he watched the house. After spending the afternoon shopping in town, he had been more than grateful for Erin's and the girls' help with unloading the car and carrying everything up those steps. His leg had been throbbing and he'd still had a hundred things to do before he could call it a night. His dinner had consisted of pure self-indulgence—junk food. After he had been released from the hospital, he'd spent four weeks living with his parents, until the constant mothering had forced him to move back to his apartment. For the next two months his sisters-in-law and mother had made daily deliveries of care packages. Even Autumn, who was living in Virginia, got into the act by signing him up for the Fruit-of-the-Month Club. Huge quantities of fresh fruit arrived on his doorstep on the tenth of every month. Which reminded him, he would have to call the company and let them know his new address. July was melon month.

He had managed to get all the food and some of his clothes put away before he called it a night. He hadn't felt like working on the depressing manuscript. With a semiwarm beer in one hand and the cane in the other, he'd gone out to the front deck and sat, watching the house as lights were turned on and off. He'd tried to visualize what was going on there, imagining bathtime with lots of bubbles, boats, and laughter. The girls would be dressed in matching little pink nightgowns with their hair all brushed and shining. They would brush their teeth, say their prayers, and slip quietly off into dreamland. Erin would then have the night to herself to indulge in her favorite television show, paint her nails, or do whatever it was mothers did when the kids were all tucked in their beds.

He figured the girls' bedrooms were at the front of the house and Erin's overlooked the lake. When he had stopped in earlier to pay the rent and give Erin his list of references, he had used the same back door they had used. He had found himself in a large, old-fashioned kitchen. None of the appliances or furnishings were new, but they were clean and neat. The kitchen table had been crowded with rows of empty glass jars, and a mass of small cucumbers had been piled on the drainboard. He'd figured Erin was going to make either a hell of a salad or pickles. Bain had never seen anyone make pickles before. He didn't think anyone still did. A quick glance into the living room had shown him neat, well-worn furniture that gleamed from a recent polishing. His daughters might not be living in the lap of luxury, but their home was tidy. Erin obviously took great pride in her home and children.

Bain's glance went involuntarily back to Erin's bedroom window. Why, when he'd purposely came out there to watch over his girls as they slept, did he worry about their mother? Who watched over Erin as she slept? Erin would instinctively hold and protect Caitlin and Arlene if they had a bad dream, but who would comfort her? Who had held her when she had lost her husband and was left with an infant and a two-year-old? Didn't she have a family who could help out? He frowned as he remembered the kitchen's dull linoleum floor, the faded exterior paint that was beginning to crack, and the surprised expressions on the girls' faces when he'd handed them a Popsicle. Erin was trying to raise the girls on a shoestring. No wonder she had been so eager to rent the apartment to the first person who came along.

Bain's eyes narrowed as he tried to figure out what to do next. He wanted to double his rent, but knew Erin wouldn't accept it. Stubborn pride was a terrible thing, and she seemed to have an abundance of it. He slowly got to his feet and climbed cautiously and quietly down the steps. His footsteps were slow and uneven as he walked along the shore of the lake and thought.

His gaze automatically returned to the house and

the huge double windows facing the lake. Erin was asleep behind them. He could just make out white lace curtains blowing inward from the cool night breeze. He wondered what Erin slept in? Satin and lace, or was there nothing between her sweet, creamy skin and the pink-rosebud sheets that had hung on the line that day? Bain moaned as his imagination kicked his body into action. For weeks he had worried that his most basic male function had been permanently damaged. He chuckled sadly as his jeans became uncomfortably tight. On one hand, it felt wonderful to be frustrated, but as the old saying on the force went, he would only be shooting blanks.

As he turned around and made his way back to the boathouse, a frown drew his eyebrows together. Why, when he was there only for his daughters, did he spend all his time thinking about their mother and wondering what her kisses would taste like? It was the worst possible thing he could be thinking about. Erin Flynn was definitely off-limits. His life was complicated enough without adding the devastating complexities that a physical relationship with Erin would bring him.

The next morning Erin started at a sudden noise. She dropped her spoon back into her bowl of cereal and stood. What in the world was all that racket? It sounded like someone was trying to demolish the boathouse.

"Mommy, what's that?" Caitlin asked.

"Who's knocking?" asked Arlene. She was too busy trying to sink a lone Cheerio in a sea of milk to bother looking up.

"It sounds like Mr. O'Neil has turned into a crazed carpenter or a mutant woodpecker." She hurried toward the back door. "Caitlin, watch Arlene, please. Mommy will be right back." She opened the door and glanced back at her younger daughter. "Arlene, don't you dare feed your breakfast to the kitten again, or there will be no dessert for you tonight."

Arlene looked up and grinned. "Kitty likes cuckoo-bird cereal."

Erin groaned. "That's not the cuckoo-bird kind of cereal. That's the nutritious stuff. The kind with ten essential vitamins and minerals to help build strong muscles."

Arlene pushed up the sleeve of her T-shirt and raised her arm. "Me got muscles. See?"

"Yes, Mommy does see, sweetie. But still, finish your breakfast. The kitty has her own food."

Arlene beamed. "Got ya'."

Erin shook her head and closed the door. Where Arlene picked up the saying "got ya'" from was a mystery. The child practically ended every conversation with those words.

She hurried off the porch and ran toward the boathouse, where the loud banging was still going on. Her feet came to a halt as she spotted Bain balanced precariously on a ladder, swinging a hammer. She could see muscles bunch under his damp T-shirt with each mighty swing of the tool. Her gaze lingered on his back before skimming over his shoulders and down his powerful arms. His forearms were tanned, and his wrists looked like steel. Intriguing, mind-boggling steel. She caught her breath and didn't speak until he'd stopped hammering. As he reached into the pouch hanging around his waist, she asked, "What are you doing?"

Bain glanced down and smiled. Lord, Erin was breathtaking in the morning light. Her long hair was twisted up into a knot on top of her head, probably in preparation for the heat of the day. If the morning temperature was any indication, today was going to be a doozie. Her cheeks were flushed, and her voice sounded huskier than he had remembered. Her light-green eyes looked even bigger with her hair pulled away from her face. A man could happily drown in those eyes. *Dangerous thoughts*, *O'Neil*. "Good morning, Erin." He glanced around the yard and frowned. "Where are those two adorable girls hiding? I hope my hammering didn't disturb you."

"The girls are eating their breakfast." She placed her hands on her hips and stared up at the steps he had been hammering on. "May I ask what you're doing?"

"You may ask me anything you like, Erin."

She smiled. "All right. Good morning, Bain. What are you doing?"

"Fixing these steps."

She squinted at the stairs. "Is there something wrong with them?"

"Nothing that a few nails and some hard pounding won't fix."

"You shouldn't be fixing them." She glanced at his leg and frowned. "I'll telephone one of those handymen, or whatever they're called, today."

Bain straightened and placed more weight on his bad leg. He had noticed her gaze. "I'm perfectly capable of hammering in some nails."

She looked embarrassed that she might have offended him. "I didn't mean to sound like you couldn't. But if I'm not mistaken, tenants don't usually do their own repairs. Weren't you supposed to complain to me or something?"

"My doctor insisted that I promise to get as much exercise as possible before he would let me leave the city. Sitting in front of a typewriter doesn't offer much in the way of exercise."

"Oh. Well, then, I'll deduct fifty dollars off your next month's rent."

"How about you invite me to Sunday night's dinner and we'll call it even?"

Erin was quiet for a minute as she studied his smile. Did it seem a little too forced? she wondered. A little too desperate? Was he that lonely? It would be wiser financially to feed Bain one meal than to deduct fifty dollars from next month's rent. Emotionally, however, she wasn't sure. It seemed too intimate to dine with one's tenant. Especially when he looked like Bain. If her dream the night before was any indication, she had been without male company too long. She mentally envisioned adding shiny new Mary Janes, white ruffled socks, and the brightest backpack she could find to Caitlin's first-day-at-school outfit. Lord, what if it was raining on the first day? Caitlin needed a new pair of boots, and a raincoat too.

Erin was already attracted to Bain and hoped she wouldn't compound the problem by going along with his suggestion. What about the feeling she had that he was hiding something? Could she have been mistaken? Maybe he was just lonely. "Would six o'clock be all right?" she asked. Her voice was small and tentative.

Bain studied the nail clutched in his fingers. "Six o'clock is fine."

She turned and started to walk back to her house.

"Erin?" She stopped and glanced over her shoulder. "I'll bring the wine."

She blinked. The last time she'd had wine with dinner was the night Cameron, the girls, and she had moved into this house. She and Cameron had split a bottle of cheap rosé over hamburgers, potato chips, and pickles. They had achieved the first step of their dreams when they'd purchased the house and surrounding acres. Cameron had wanted to start his own landscaping business. He was to do the hard manual work while she stayed home, raised the children, and grew the flowers and shrubs in the greenhouses. Within two weeks of their obtaining the mortgage, Cameron had fallen ill. Erin had been left with five acres of lakefront property, six broken-down greenhouses, and shattered dreams. It had taken her two years of hard struggles and sacrifices to know she still wanted the nursery business. On her own she maintained three out of the six greenhouses and sold flowers and some small shrubs to several florists in nearby towns. It was time to reach for the dreams again, but this time they would be her dreams.

"Make it red wine," she said. A determined little smile teased the corners of her lips as she walked back to her house. It was time to start living again.

Such thoughts were put aside, though, as she

heard Caitlin shouting something at Arlene. She knew once again that she was about to rescue the kitchen from the destruction and calamity that usually occurred whenever she left her children alone.

Bain's thoughtful gaze followed Erin as she hurried into her house. Something was making her wary of him. Was he pushing too hard? Going too fast? Was his desperation to be a part of his family showing? Frowning he turned back to the steps and started to pound in another nail.

The girls' shrieks of delight finally penetrated Bain's concentration. He looked up from the battered portable typewriter and peered out the sliding screen door toward the lake. The only thing he could see was a faraway sailboat, sparkling water, and the outline of the distant shore. He cautiously got to his feet and massaged the cramped muscles in his leg. He had been sitting in the same position too long. A neat pile of six typed pages sat beside him, with a seventh page still rolled into the typewriter.

Somewhere in the corner of the room, in a pile of boxes still unpacked, was the original manuscript he had been working on back in New York City. He hated the story, but more importantly he hated the man he had had to become in order to write such a thing. Where were the hope, the dreams, the colors?

With her sweetness and friendliness, Erin was already showing him the colors that still existed in the world. He could no longer write in black-and-white with endless corridors of gray. He wanted the vivid hues of happiness, sorrow, goodness, evil, love, and even hate. He wanted to write in the intense colors of hopes and dreams.

Bain made his way over to the door and breathed in the fresh air filtering through the screen. As Caitlin's laugh filled the air, he glanced down at the shoreline. Caitlin and Arlene were sitting at the lake's edge wiggling their legs in the water. Erin was farther out with the glimmering waters lapping at her thighs. The cuffs of her khaki shorts were showing signs of moisture where the water teased the material. It looked like the Flynn women were taking some time to enjoy the afternoon.

Bain's fingers went to the snap of his jeans. Within seconds he was pulling off his sticky T-shirt and dropping it next to the discarded jeans. He had to go through four boxes before he found a pair of cut-off denim shorts. The doctor had said exercise, and swimming was one of the best forms of exercise known to man.

Erin was trying to lure Arlene into the lake with promises of safety and coolness. As usual Arlene wasn't buying it. She was perfectly content to sit at the edge of the lake and splash around in the ankle-deep water. "Come on, honey. Mommy won't drop you, I promise."

"No."

"Please?"

"No. Bad fishies are in there." Arlene turned her attention back to the yellow plastic boat bobbing at her feet.

One of these days Erin was going to kill her brother, Patrick. He had meant well when he had visited that spring and tried to warn the girls about the dangers of the lake. But did he have to mention the fact that fish lived in the lake? Arlene, with her vivid imagination, placed the sharks, octopuses, and eels from Caitlin's animal dictionary book into the lake. It had taken Erin half the summer to get Arlene to sit and play at the water's edge. By the way things were going, Arlene would be in high school before she learned to swim.

A movement off to the side caught her attention. She glanced toward the boathouse and bit the inside of her cheek to keep from groaning. Bain was walking toward them, and by the way he was dressed, he was either going swimming or America was suffering from a severe denim shortage. He was shirtless, and a battered and worn pair of cutoffs rode low on his hips, giving her an enticing view of muscles, crisp dark hairs, and enough tanned skin to bring back censorship. A cream-colored towel was draped around his neck, its fringed ends drawing her gaze to his trim waist. Her startled gaze shot back up to his devastating smile, and she remembered the dream from last night. Just thinking about his dream kisses could melt the silver fillings in her teeth.

"Hi, Erin . . . Caitlin." He bent down and hesitantly ruffled a handful of fine baby-soft orange curls. "And Arlene." He was rewarded with a brilliant smile. He straightened and grinned at Erin. "Hot one today, isn't it?"

Erin felt a bead of perspiration slip down her neck and into the cleavage between her breasts. Bain could generate more heat than an exploding volcano and be twice as deadly. "It should be cooling down soon. They're predicting showers this evening."

Bain had watched that tiny drop of moisture disappear into the shadowy crevice and silently cursed his body's reaction. He quickly dropped the cane and towel down next to a small pile of plastic containers. Scanning the labels, he saw that all were sunscreen lotions and blocks. Five bottles and three people?

He looked back up at Erin. "Are you expecting company?" It hadn't occurred to him, until that minute, that Erin might have a boyfriend. After all, she was gorgeous, and a respectable amount of time had passed since her husband had passed away.

"Afraid not," she said, chuckling. "They're all ours. Did you want to borrow some?"

He released the breath he had been holding. "Never use the stuff."

"Arlene and I would burn to a crisp without at least a number thirty."

"I don't burn at all."

"You're just like Caitlin, then. I swear, the child wouldn't need any at all if I wasn't so worried about the depleting ozone layers. A person can't be too careful nowadays."

Bain's gaze riveted on Caitlin as she dashed about in knee-deep water, making as many waves and splashes as she could. Caitlin had inherited his coloring! What else could he have given the girls without noticing?

"Mommy, Caitlin splashing me," Arlene yelled.

"Caitlin, please don't splash your sister, and Arlene, you didn't have to yell. I'm standing right here."

Bain hid his smile as Caitlin danced a wee bit closer to her younger sister before moving away. His mother always said that trouble usually comes in threes. She should meet Caitlin and Arlene. Now there was double trouble if he ever saw it. He took a step into the lake and shivered as the chilly water covered his calves. He glanced at Erin's shorts and skimpy tank top. "Aren't you going swimming?"

"No." A tide of red swept up her cheeks. "You go ahead. The water feels great."

Bain stepped deeper into the water. When it was waist deep, he turned to wave at the girls. He was momentarily thrown off balance by their expressions. Both looked at him with such wonder that he glanced down at his bare chest. No blue tights, no red cape, no big *S* printed across his chest. So why were they looking at him as if he were Superman? He waved once before he dove into the lake.

He surfaced a good fifteen yards from the shore and waved at the girls, who were shading their eyes and searching the lake. Caitlin clapped her hands and waved back, Erin gave a slight nod, and Arlene was wiping at something on her face. With powerful strokes he started to swim parallel to the shore.

Twenty minutes later he left the water and sat down near his towel and Erin. He knew he shouldn't have stayed so long in the water, but Caitlin's constant cheering had inspired him to show off a little. He was going to pay for his folly that night.

"You did it, Bain!" Caitlin exclaimed. "You must have swum a hundred miles."

Bain chuckled and teasingly pulled at her ponytail. "Not quite, love. But thanks for the vote of confidence." He looked over at Erin and frowned. Arlene's face was buried against her breasts, and she appeared to be crying. "What's the matter with Arlene?"

"She thought you were going to be eaten by a shark."

"A shark?"

Arlene lifted her tear-streaked face and hesitantly turned toward Bain. A glimmer of a smile teased the corners of her mouth when she saw that Bain was indeed all right. "Fishies no eat you?"

"No, honey, the fish didn't bother me." He gently wiped at a lone tear glistening on her cheek. "Who told you there were sharks in the lake?"

"Uncle Pat."

"My brother," Erin said. "He was trying to warn the girls of all the dangers of living so close to the lake. He was worried one of them would go out too far and drown." She looked down at Arlene, still cradled in her arms. "Little one here took it to heart. She thinks every sea creature known to man, and a few that aren't, live in our lake."

Bain nodded with understanding. "There's only one way to show Arlene what actually lives in the lake." He tickled the end of her adorable upturned nose with the damp fringes of his towel.

Huge green eyes the same color as Erin's stared back at him. "How?"

"We have to go fishing."

Both girls turned to their mother. Erin tried to ignore their pleading expressions as she repeated, "Fishing?"

"When I went looking for a ladder this morning, I noticed you have a couple of poles hanging in the boathouse."

"They were left there by the previous owner."

"I could clean them up and get them working."

Erin released Arlene and stood up. "I don't know, Bain. It sounds dangerous." She brushed at the dirt covering her rear.

Bain swallowed hard as his gaze followed the movement of her hand. He quickly got to his feet. "We'll be fishing for trout or bass, not great whites."

She started picking up the kids' toys and bottles of sunscreen. "But what if we fall in?"

"Then you get wet." He chuckled at the horrified expression on her face. "Don't worry, I'm sure I can hunt up some life jackets for the girls if you're that worried."

She was silent, studying the label on the plastic bottle clutched in her hand as if she had never seen it before.

"Mommy will need one too," Caitlin said.

Bain stared at Erin, understanding slowly dawning. "You can't swim, can you?"

Erin shoved the bottle into a canvas tote bag. "It's not that I can't. It's just that I never had the opportunity to learn."

"But you live right on a lake."

"Who do you think was going to teach me? Arlene or Caitlin? From what I understand, a person could drown if the first self-taught lesson fails."

"Would you like me to teach you and the girls to swim?"

Caitlin's face lit up as she excitedly pulled on the hem of her mother's tank top. Arlene looked decidedly scared by the entire idea as she backed up another foot from the lake's edge. Erin studied her younger daughter for a moment, then turned back to Bain. "What would you charge?"

"Nothing."

"I can't expect you to teach all of us for nothing."

Bain saw that stubborn look creep over her face. Damn it all, Erin was going to drive him crazy with her pride and independence. "For every lesson I give, you can bake me a pie, a cake, a batch of cookies, or something else good to eat." She arched one delicate eyebrow, and he smiled. "I have a sweet tooth that store-bought junk food just doesn't satisfy."

Erin laughed. "Your mother must have had her hands full with you."

"After my three older brothers, she was ready for anything."

"Four boys?"

He nodded. "And I must not have been too bad, because I have a younger sister." He glanced at Caitlin. "You know, my mom's name is Caitlin too?"

"Really?" Caitlin said. "What's she like?"

Bain was momentarily silent as he studied Caitlin's face. "I would say she was just like you when she was a little girl. She had red wavy hair like you, except now it has a few well-deserved gray highlights." He brushed a finger across her cheek. "She also has the same dusting of freckles."

Caitlin's grin brightened. "Is she a nice mommy?"

"The best." Bain glanced at Erin and hastily corrected himself. "I mean *one* of the best." Erin's blush caused him to lose his train of thought. The tide of red started at the low neckline of her top and swept clear up to her hairline. In that moment he would have sold his soul to know exactly where that blush started.

She turned away as if in embarrassment. "Come on, girls, it's time to start dinner."

Bain was intrigued by her sudden desire to leave. "Did you want to start those lessons tomorrow?"

She paused, then said, "No, Monday will be soon enough." Erin wasn't looking forward to her first lesson. She didn't know which would be worse, making a fool of herself trying to swim or being in such close bodily contact with Bain. If it wasn't for Arlene, she would call off the entire lesson.

Bain sensed her hesitance and wondered at it. She obviously wasn't afraid of the water, or she wouldn't have gone wading in it. Was she fearful of too much contact with him? Fearful, perhaps, because she felt the same strong tug of attraction as he did?

He shrugged off his hope-filled thoughts and said, "No problem. Monday it is." He smiled down at the girls and playfully teased their hair. "I'll see you two tomorrow night, if not sooner."

Both girls waved and called good-bye as they followed their mother across the yard and into their house.

He stood in the brilliant sunshine and felt suddenly alone. Each of the little lasses had dragged a piece of his heart behind them, but it was Erin's absence that caused the loneliness. He wanted to be more than just a tenant or a swimming coach to her. How much more, he wasn't sure. He only knew he wanted more.

THREE

Bain stood at the foot of the stairs in Erin's home and chuckled at the commotion taking place in the upstairs bathroom. Erin presumably was given the girls their bath, but by the sound of things the girls were flooding the entire second floor.

Erin's voice suddenly carried through the house. "Arlene, I said *in* the bathtub!" One of the girl's high-pitched squeals followed, along with a muttering that sounded like Erin praying for something. His chuckle grew louder as he walked back into the kitchen. Blood definitely would tell.

Dirty dishes were piled all over the counter, and messy pots covered the stove. Erin had mistakenly thought he would leave immediately after eating the delicious Sunday dinner she'd prepared. No way was he leaving her this mess after she had cooked all day.

While she gave the kids their bath, he would start on the kitchen.

He glanced around the room and frowned. No dishwasher, no microwave, and he knew there wasn't a clothes dryer. How in the hell did she get everything done without the simple basics of life? What was she, a modern-day pioneer woman?

Ten minutes later Erin entered the kitchen and froze. Bain was elbow deep in suds and he was singing, of all things, the jingle from a television commercial advertising cars. Clean dishes were piled high in the plastic rack ready to be dried. Without being asked, he had dug right in and started the dishes. More of her initial wariness with Bain dissolved as his hold on her heart squeezed a little tighter. Not only was he gorgeous to look at and had a gift for storytelling, but he was obviously housebroken. Bain O'Neil was just too good to be true.

"Mommy, Mommy, can we have dessert now?" Caitlin and Arlene yelled as they ran into the room.

Bain turned around and grinned at the now-clean girls. "Erin, quick, there're two strange kids in the house!"

Erin lovingly gazed at her daughters and smiled. Their red hair gleamed under the harsh kitchen light, and the freckles dusting Caitlin's nose were more noticeable without the layer of dust that usually covered her face. Arlene's nose and cheeks were tinted pink from the sun. How the sun rays had penetrated the dirt Arlene always wore with such ease was a total mystery. "I know. They come in here every night about this time and beg for goodies." Erin watched as both girls giggled and moved closer to Bain. He had won them over that evening with tales of fairies and leprechauns. If the truth was to be known, he had kept Erin herself on the edge of her seat more than once waiting for the outcome of his tale.

"What shall we do?" Bain asked her.

"We could either feed them"—both girls giggled some more—"or send them back where they came from."

Bain made a big show of frowning while considering the idea. "I think we should send them back where they came from."

"I say we give them a huge piece of peach pie before sending them off to bed." Erin hid her smile as the girls glanced from Bain to her, then back to Bain.

After wiping his wet hands on a towel, Bain scratched his head, stared up at the ceiling, then snapped his fingers. "I've got it! I'll throw a coin up in the air. Heads they go back to wherever, tails it's peach pie." He pulled a coin from his jeans' pocket and flipped it high into the air. All eyes were upon it as he caught it and slapped it onto the back of his other hand. He made a production out of slowly removing his top hand to reveal the coin underneath. "It's tails!"

Both girls cheered with delight.

Bain glanced at Erin, and his expression changed from teasing to intense as his gaze slid over her. She had debated what to wear that night, finally choosing a soft yellow dress with a flowing skirt and a rounded neckline that just hinted at the curves of her breasts. She felt her body heating as his gaze lingered at that neckline, then he snapped it back up to her face.

"I guess that means they get pie after all," he said, his voice a little rough.

"I guess it does." She pulled down some plates and placed the pie on the table. "Did you want a piece, Bain?"

"I'll take mine after I finish up these dishes and the girls go up to bed." He smiled at her and turned back to the waiting pots and pans.

Erin studied the crisp golden crust of the pie sitting in front of her. The rules of the evening had just changed. The look Bain had given her a minute ago was not the look of a tenant or even a friend. It was the look of a male with something more than peach pie on his mind. She tried to squash the flash of excitement that surged through her as she sliced into the pie. She must have been mistaken, she told herself. Bain was her tenant. The last thing she should be doing was having lusty thoughts about him. She didn't want to run the poor man off before he even got unpacked. And what about the feeling she occasionally got that he was hiding something?

Bain sighed in relief as he set the tray containing Erin's and his pie and coffee on a small table on the front porch. Erin sat in a rocking chair, and he dropped down in another one on the opposite side of the table. Peace and quiet was the only sound he could hear, and he contentedly breathed in the fresh, cool night air. The dishes were finally done, and after two more stories the girls were tucked into their beds. He glanced at the woman silently rocking beside him. "It's strange out here, isn't it?"

"In what way?" she asked as she handed him the plate with the bigger piece of pie.

"The silence." He glanced out over the neatly trimmed yard. Arlene and Caitlin had left their bikes and a rusty old wagon parked beneath a giant maple tree. "I stayed awake half the night last night listening to the silence."

"I sleep with the window open or cracked, even in the dead of winter, just to hear the wind blow. In the spring you can practically hear the leaves growing, and in the summer their gentle rustling is so calming. The fall's my favorite, with the crackling of leaves and the crisp cold nights. The winter's the eeriest, but the most compelling. The wind roars over the lake and whistles through the barren trees like a train bound for hell and taking no passengers."

Bain was momentarily thrown off balance by her uncharacteristic remark. "Do you read a lot of Stephen King?"

She laughed. "No. The silence used to unnerve me when I first moved here. I was so used to sleeping with the sounds of sirens wailing, horns blaring, and the constant noise of a city that I needed the diversion. The wind became my distraction."

Bain was silent as they ate their pie. Erin was as lonely as he was, he mused. Even with the girls, she still needed the comforting sound of the wind. Be it gentle or howling, the wind gave her a sense of security. "I heard a couple of birds and other night animals."

"Wait until the Canadian geese make their way south this fall. It might just shoot your peace-and-quiet theory." She placed her empty plate on the tray and reached for her coffee. "Can I ask you a question?"

"Sure."

"What would you have done about the girls if the coin had landed on heads?"

He chuckled and pulled the coin out of his pocket

again. He handed it across the table to her. In the faint light coming from the living-room window, she could see it was tails. "So?"

"Turn it over."

Erin turned it over and laughed. It was tails on both sides of the coin. "You cheated."

"Nope, just playing the odds." He repocketed the coin. "I win more bets with my nieces and nephews this way."

"I imagine you do." She studied Bain's profile in the pale light. It contained a strength of character she didn't normally see in men. She could well understand him becoming a cop. She glanced down at his leg and shuddered, thinking what his injury must have cost him. Suddenly realizing he hadn't brought his cane, she glanced up and said, "You're not using your cane."

"I'm trying to use it less and less each day."

"Is it safe to do that?"

"Well, I haven't fallen flat on my face yet. If you notice my nose bandaged one day, be polite and don't laugh."

Erin liked a man who could laugh at himself, but she was afraid she was beginning to like Bain a little too much. Her emotions seemed to have been on fast-forward since he had shown up on her doorstep. "I guess it's time to call it a night."

If he was surprised by her sudden desire to end

the evening, he didn't show it. He got to his feet and reached for the tray.

"Here, I'll take that," she said.

"I can manage."

"But what about your leg?"

He glanced down at the tray. "If I do fall flat on my face, I guess I'm going to owe you for some dishes."

She followed as he walked the length of the wraparound porch and through the back kitchen door. "There," he said as he carefully placed the tray on the counter. "Safe and sound."

"Thank you, Bain," she said with slight sarcasm. "I don't know how I would have managed without you."

"Sassy *and* spirited," Bain said as he slowly walked toward her. He ignored the voice of caution screaming in his head. The temptation to taste such an explosive combination was too much.

"Are you talking about me or a racehorse?" she asked.

"You, lass. Definitely you." He raised his hand and caressed her smooth cheek with a lone finger. Her skin felt like creamy satin. Her trembling mouth looked lush and red, simply begging to be taken. "Will I receive an eviction notice if I kiss you once?"

"Once?"

He leaned in closer and traced her lips with his finger. "Make it twice." Her lips parted on a sigh. "But then again . . ." His mouth settled on hers as his fingers slid into the thick braid at the back of her head.

Erin sighed against the sweetness of his kiss, and every doubt she had harbored about Bain disintegrated into a pool of desire. Her arms automatically encircled his neck and pulled her closer. This was the sweet, gentle kiss from her dreams the other night.

Bain felt every nerve ending in his body snap alive as Erin pressed herself against him. He wanted her with an intensity that shook him clean down to his foundation. Need, desire, passion, and hunger struggled against his better sense, trying to dominate it. Colors were exploding all around him. He fought for control but lost it when Erin lightly nipped at his lower lip.

In a flash he had her pressed against the kitchen wall and was devouring her with feverish kisses. The more he demanded, the more she gave. His arousal nearly peaked when he cupped one of her plump breasts in his hand and felt the hardened nipple against his palm. He released her mouth and forged a blazing trail of kisses down her slender neck. He could feel the fierce pounding of her blood as he neared the barrier of her dress. Clothes became unimportant as he captured the hard peak of her nipple through the material of her dress and bra.

She purred in ecstasy as she arched her back and pulled his head closer. Need exploded in Bain with more power than a nuclear bomb. It was incinerating time and reason, annihilating caution. He fought the effects of Erin's influence and lifted his head. In a daze he slowly opened his eyes and groaned. Erin had totally surrendered to the feverish passion that was consuming them both. With her head thrown back, her breathing fast and unsteady, her fingers digging into his shoulders, trying to tug him closer, Erin was a woman on the verge of surrender. He was tempted, so tempted, to satisfy their aching bodies, but what about tomorrow?

He had come there for a glimpse of his children and had stayed because of their mother. He couldn't risk throwing his change at true happiness away in the heat of a moment.

Bain dropped his arms from around her, releasing her. Guilt ridden by the look of confusion clouding her face, he stepped away and leaned his forehead against the wall. He concentrated on counting his huge gulps of air until his breathing returned halfway to normal. Hearing Erin move away, he turned and faced her. She'd put half the distance of the room between them.

He noticed the flush staining her cheeks and the

defensive way she crossed her arms over her breasts, trying to cover the dampness left by his mouth. He closed his eyes in anguish. Lord, how he wanted her! "I'm sorry, Erin."

"For what?" she asked, her voice trembling.

"I didn't mean to go so far." He jammed his fingers through his hair. "I only wanted to kiss you good night and see if you tasted as good as you look."

She arched one eyebrow.

He saw the question she refused to ask burning in her gaze and smiled. "Better, Erin, much better than I ever imagined."

Her pink cheeks turned crimson. "Thank you, I think."

"You're welcome." He stayed against the wall and rammed his hands into his pockets. She still looked confused, flustered, and totally kissable. He needed to touch her. He moved closer, and his hand shook as he traced the delicate curve of her jaw. "Lord, how I want you."

"Then why did you stop?" Her brows drew together in a worried frown. "There's no *Mrs*. O'Neil stashed away someplace is there?"

He stepped back, looking at her in surprise. "There're a lot of Mrs. O'Neils, but none of them happen to be my wife, if that is what you're getting at." He scowled. "I already told you I wasn't married."

"It wouldn't have been the first time a man had lied to a woman." She smiled faintly. "Sorry, but I have this thing against liars."

Bain strode over to the window and pushed the curtains aside to stare out into the night. He rubbed the back of his neck. Oh, what a tangled web this was turning out to be. He'd known he should have kept his distance. "You do?"

"I watched my parents' and too many of my friends' marriages end up in divorce because there wasn't total honesty between them. I believe honesty is the foundation for any relationship."

He couldn't help but smile as he turned to face her. "Are we going to have a relationship?"

"Do you think I go around kissing everyone that way?"

He scowled again. "I should hope not." On edge, he started pacing over the worn linoleum. He'd known from the beginning this would never work out. Erin was speaking about relationships and honesty. The relationship he could give her, but honesty was the million-dollar question. How would she handle being told he was the "sperm donor"?

He stopped pacing and studied her face. "What if being totally honest hurts someone?"

"As in someone you love?"

"Yes."

"If the foundation crumbles and falls because one person was being honest with the other, then the relationship wasn't meant to be." She looked curiously at him. "Is there something you're not telling me?"

"There're a lot of things I'm not telling you." He grinned and slowly walked over to her.

"Like what?"

"Like, did you know your hair is a mess?" He twirled a loose curl around his finger and gently tugged.

She chuckled. "Maybe this honesty thing isn't all it's cracked up to be."

His thumb grazed her cheekbone before trailing down her jaw and over her chin. "Ah . . . and your lips."

"What's wrong with them?"

"Absolutely nothing." He skimmed his thumb over the soft lower lip. "They are absolutely perfect." He replaced his thumb with his mouth.

The kiss quickly escalated to volcanic proportions, and Bain released Erin before he lost control. Kissing her again had been a mistake, he thought as he stalked back over to the window and glared out into the darkness. "That's the problem," he said. "Every time I see them, I want to taste them."

She laughed again. "I can see where that might be a problem."

He gripped the windowsill to keep himself from racing back across the room to her. "I think we should think about it some more before we go any farther."

"Well, who died and left you boss?" she snapped.

He would have laughed if the situation wasn't so grave. He'd thought she would be appreciative that he had called a halt, giving her some time to think things through. Instead she was getting mad. Erin Flynn boasted more gumption than a thoroughbred racehorse. One corner of his mouth tilted up as he faced her. "Like I said before, sassy and spirited."

"Bain O'Neil, I don't like being compared to horses."

He opened the door and chuckled. "Then stop acting so mule-headed." He blew a kiss across the room and winked. "We will continue this fascinating conversation tomorrow night after the girls are in bed."

Erin threw a pot holder at the closing door. "The devil himself will be building a snowman in hell before I sleep with you, Bain O'Neil!"

Bain's voice floated back in through the open windows as he jumped off the porch. "Oh, Erin, love, sleep is the last thing I want to do with you."

FOUR

The next afternoon Erin continued to kneel beside the lake talking to Arlene as Caitlin rushed over to greet Bain. Erin purposely kept her back to him as she patiently explained to Arlene for the fourth time about the swimming lessons.

"Bain, Bain!" Caitlin yelled. "Is it time now?"

"Yes, honey, it's time for your swimming lesson." He stopped beside Erin. "I see you have your mother's patience—none."

Erin looked up at him and glared. The man was pushing his luck to the limit. She'd had a total of two hours of sleep the night before and wasn't in the mood for another round of frustration with Mr. I-Know-What's-Good-For-You Kiss-and-Run O'Neil. "Well, well, look who finally woke up," she said. "Did the big old bright sun disturb you?"

He chuckled and tossed Caitlin up in the air.

Catching the laughing child, he smiled down at Erin. "A man's got to work, lass."

Erin stood up and lightly brushed at the seat of her new bathing suit. She hadn't been able to resist going out the day before and buying the girls and herself bathing suits. Caitlin looked adorable in a light green two-piece suit while Arlene couldn't have been cuter in a darker green one-piece suit with black dots and pink ruffles around the waist. Hers was a one-piece mint-green number that had promised to slim her waist and accent her better features, and it did. After the delivery of the girls her once firm and flat tummy had never quite returned to its original shape. By the interested gleam in Bain's eyes she would say the suit had done its job admirably.

She reached down and squeezed Arlene's hand in reassurance. "Which one of the girls do you want to teach first?"

Bain winked at Arlene. "Neither, Erin. I was planning on teaching you first. Arlene might feel a whole lot more comfortable if she sees you learn first."

"Me?" She hadn't meant to sound so anxious in front of the girls, but "chicken" could have been her middle name.

"Yes, you. Unless you've changed your mind?"

She glanced at her two daughters, who were

staring up at her, and conceded defeat. "No, no. I'm perfectly happy to go first. I want them to see just how easy it will be." She smiled at the girls and turned her attention to Bain. "What do I do first?"

He looked as if he had a thousand different answers to that question, none of which he could say in front of her daughters. "First," he said, "we go out about waist deep and you float on your back." He looked at Caitlin and Arlene. "You two stay right here. You can play with your boats or watch your Mommy and me."

Erin walked out into the lake until the water was lapping at her waist. She turned and waved to Arlene, who was standing wide-eyed at the shoreline clutching her two plastic boats, then looked at Bain, standing beside her. "Now what?"

"You lie flat on your back and leave the rest up to me."

Erin cursed her fair complexion as a tide of red swept up her face. She tried to ignore the teasing lights in his eyes by looking down. However, she found herself staring at a rock-hard bronze chest covered with dark auburn curls. She studied the tiny beads of moisture, kicked up by his walk out into the lake, clinging to those mesmerizing curls. Her tongue slowly moistened her lower lip. "What if I go under?"

"I'll save you."

There was a roughness to his voice, and her gaze shot up to meet his. "You will?"

"Oh, Erin." He groaned. "You don't think I'd let you drown, do you?"

"Well, the thought may have crossed your mind."

"Many thoughts of you cross my mind, but drowning you isn't one of them." He lightly tapped the tip of her nose. "Now, lie back."

She glanced hesitantly at the dark-blue water behind her. It did look as sinister as Arlene imagined it to be. Maybe there were sharks in it after all. Whoever had had the idea of swimming lessons should be shot. "Now?"

Bain chuckled and placed a hand at the middle of her back, his fingers spreading out across her skin. "Lean backward. I've got you."

As she leaned backward into the water, she yelped as his other hand cupped her bottom. "What in the hell do you think you're doing?" she whispered fiercely.

"Keeping you from drowning. Now, relax."

She glared up at him. Having his hand cupping her bottom was one surefire way to keep her from not relaxing. But, she realized, her arms were out to her sides and the water was gently lapping at her body. She was floating! "You can let me go now."

"Not until you relax your muscles."

"My muscles *are* relaxed! You can let me go

now." His warm hands pressed against her body were a greater threat than the water.

He shook his head and grinned. "As you wish." He lowered his hands a good ten inches.

Erin felt herself going under and grabbed the only available object—Bain.

With no thought except to keep herself from drowning, Erin plastered herself against his chest. Bain apparently had other thoughts, though. He wrapped his arms around her, holding her securely, and she pressed herself closer into his embrace. Her fears dissipated as one of his large hands spanned her rib cage while the other arm cradled her legs. Warm fingers stroked the back of her thigh below the water. She kept her face buried in the curve of his neck as his fingers teased the edge of her suit. Her teeth nipped lightly at the hammering pulse in his neck as his fingers tried to slip under the clinging material.

"Mommy!" Caitlin yelled.

Both Erin and Bain looked toward shore and saw Caitlin standing knee deep in the water. Arlene was still watching from the shore. "Yes, honey?" Erin called as she released her death grip on Bain's neck.

"Why aren't you swimming?"

Erin turned beet red and refused to look at a choking Bain. She wiggled out of his hold and backed away from him. "The first step to swimming is floating on your back, honey. Mommy has to learn to do that first, then it's your turn, okay?"

"Okay." Caitlin turned back to the shore and picked up her boats.

Erin frowned at Bain. The man looked to be torn between laughter and pain. "Let's try this again, shall we?"

He controlled his laughter and solemnly held out his hand toward her back. She leaned backward into the water nicely, but stiffened again when his hand cupped her bottom. "Erin, you have to relax, or you will never float."

"How do you expect me to relax when your hand is *there*?" she whispered.

He moved his hand lower, to her thighs, and grinned. "Better?"

"No!" At least when he held her bottom, her bathing suit was between his warm fingers and her skin.

He sighed and moved his hand back to her derriere. "Close your eyes and think of something tranquil."

She closed her eyes and muttered an old Irish oath her grandfather had unintentionally taught her when she was a little girl.

Bain chuckled. "Sounds kinky to me, but I'm game if you are."

She kept her eyes closed and refused to blush.

She should have known he would understand that saying. Trying to forget him, she focused all her concentration on some serene white-sand beach with only a gentle breeze and surf for company. She added swaying palm trees and a few colorful birds to her island. A huge green beach blanket and a yellow-and-white-striped umbrella joined the scene. Was that a bottle of champagne sticking out from a bucket of ice? Why were there two glasses?

Bain gazed down at the dreamy expression on Erin's face. He would have given away the first draft of his book to know what she was thinking. Slowly he lowered his hands and smiled as Erin stayed afloat. Stepping back, he frantically waved at Caitlin and Arlene.

Erin saw herself lying on the blanket reaching for someone. She smiled as Bain started to lower himself onto her.

"Mommy! Mommy! You did it!"

Erin heard her daughters' cheers, and the vision abruptly ended. Every muscle in her body stiffened, and she sank like a stone.

Bain hauled her back up and spun her around in a circle. "You were doing it, lass."

She caught her breath and pushed the strands of wet hair that had escaped her braid out of her face. "I was?"

"You sure were." He started to walk toward

shore still carrying her. "Tell her, girls. Wasn't she floating all by herself?"

"You were, Mommy," Caitlin said.

"Bain had his hands way up in the air," added Arlene, mimicking his waving.

Erin muttered something under her breath about his hands, but he couldn't quite make it out. When he reached dry land, he lowered her to the ground, grateful he hadn't lost his balance and made a complete fool of himself. His leg wasn't quite up to carrying her and walking yet. "Did you say something, Erin?"

"I said it must be time for Caitlin and Arlene's turn."

Erin watched as Caitlin threw herself into Bain's arms. Her daughter instinctively knew she would find safety and strength there. She smiled and waved to Caitlin as Bain carried her a couple of yards out into the lake.

Turning to Arlene, Erin sighed. Arlene had backed up another two steps from the water's edge. Teaching Arlene to swim was going to take more than patience, it was going to take love and understanding.

"Come on, honey, I'll make a deal with you." She held out her hand toward her daughter. "If you let me carry you out there to where Bain and Caitlin are, you don't have to float on your back. You can just hang on to me and watch Caitlin, okay?"

Arlene's anxious gaze darted back and forth between Bain, Caitlin, and Erin. "Really?"

"Honest Injun." Erin held out her arms and waited.

Arlene stepped into the embrace and wrapped her little arms around her mother's neck. "No swim with fishies."

Erin stood up and slowly walked toward Bain. "Not today, honey."

Arlene's arms clung tighter as the water grew deeper. "Got ya'."

Bain glanced up from Caitlin and smiled at Arlene and Erin. They looked so much alike, he thought. They had mother and daughter stamped on them from the top of their blazing hair to the soles of their petite feet. Caitlin favored his side of the family more with her suntanned skin, freckles, and deeper shade of hair. Anyone looking at them now would automatically think they were a family.

Hell, they were one, only not all of them knew it.

Erin heard Bain's footsteps on the wooden porch as he approached the kitchen door. The steady rhythm of the sharp knife she was using to slice beets never faltered as the soft knock sounded on the screen door. Without turning from the drainboard, she called, "Come on in, Bain."

She had been half hoping and half dreading he would come. After tucking Caitlin and Arlene into bed for the night, she had debated changing into something more alluring than her faded cotton dress, but had squashed the idea when she'd opened her closet door. Her three "best" dresses were as sensual as nun's habits, and the only piece of lingerie she owned was the now-yellowed peignoir set from her honeymoon eight years earlier. Who was she trying to fool? Seduction wasn't hanging in her closet or even in her budget. With a sad little laugh, she had quietly closed the closet door and gone down to the kitchen. She had two bushel baskets filled with beets to preserve.

Bain stopped dead as he entered the kitchen and glanced around. What in the heck was she doing with enough beets to feed a Third World country? He lowered the two crystal champagne glasses to the table and pushed aside a couple of huge beets to make room for the chilled bottle of champagne he had brought with him. Talk about being on two different wavelengths. That afternoon he had been positive he had read the signs right. Erin wanted him as much as he wanted her. It had been in her body movements, the way she flushed every time he touched her. More importantly, he had seen it in her eyes—heat so intense, he'd been amazed Lake Cayuga hadn't dried up during their swimming lesson.

Over a solitary dinner in his cramped, lonely apartment, he had carried on a running argument with his conscience. He was physically attracted to Erin, but he had been attracted to women before. So why this desperation? Why the chilled champagne, the sleepless nights, the perpetual arousal? Was it all generated by Erin the woman, or was it Erin the mother of his children? Was she the answer to his dreams of a loving wife and family, or were the children the answer, and Erin was very conveniently fitting in? The truth had been more elusive than the taste of his frozen dinner. He had ended up throwing out the uneaten dinner, wolfing down half a bag of chocolate chip cookies, and taking a quick shower.

He walked up behind Erin and peered over her shoulder. "What are you doing?"

He felt her shiver as his breath caressed her neck. "Canning beets."

He glanced at the sink filled with beets ready to be washed. With a sigh he picked up the vegetable brush and started to scrub.

"What are you doing?"

He grinned. "Canning beets."

"Why?"

"Because that's obviously what you want to do tonight." He handed her a clean beet and picked up the next dirty one.

Erin stared at the vegetable as if she'd never seen a beet before in her life. He thought she wanted to can beets when there was a gorgeous, curl-your-stomach, hot-diggity man in her kitchen? Was Bain out of his mind? Granted, she had been canning beets, but that wasn't what she *wanted* to do. She glanced from Bain, who was joyfully scrubbing another beet, to the bottle of champagne sitting on the table. He obviously hadn't had canning on his mind either. She sliced up another beet and dumped it into a waiting mason jar. A scowl darkened her expression as Bain happily handed her the next beet. Sighing dramatically, she wiped her brow. "Boy, canning can sure make a person thirsty."

Bain stifled a chuckle as he placed two more clean beets on the drainboard. "I'll get us something." He wiped his hands and ceremoniously popped open the bottle of champagne. When he'd filled both glasses, he handed one to Erin. He lightly touched the rim of his glass to hers. "To beets."

She blinked. "To beets?" It was hardly the toast she had been expecting. Whatever happened to "To us," or "To the gorgeous color of your eyes," or even "To a prosperous relationship"? To waste expensive champagne on a toast to beets was sacrilegious.

She watched Bain sip from his glass and replace it on the table. He scooped up another handful of beets and dumped them into the sink. "I'll have you know," he said, "I'm becoming very fond of these little critters."

A groan rose to her throat and lodged there. Bain was completely off his rocker. The girls were asleep, the night was cooling down, and they were generating enough heat in the kitchen to hard-boil every egg in her refrigerator.

"I'll make sure I save you a jar," she said as she picked up the knife and started to slash at the next beet.

"Where did you get all of these, anyway? I don't remember seeing any vegetable garden, just hundreds of flowers and plants."

"Mr. Jacobson down the road stopped by this afternoon and traded me two baskets of beets for a floral arrangement for his wife. It's their seventeenth wedding anniversary today. They don't have a lot of money, but he had some extra beets."

Bain stared down at the purplish beet in his hand. "Is that how you support yourself, by trading flowers for food?"

"No." She dumped a cut-up beet into a jar and reached for the next one. "I sell flowers, plants, and some shrubs to florists in the surrounding towns. Some of the local farmers stop by occasionally and swap whatever vegetables or fruits are in season for a few flowers."

Bain held out another clean beet. When she reached for the vegetable, he refused to let it go. His gaze locked with hers. "I couldn't help but notice that only half of the greenhouses have anything in them."

Erin felt her teeth clench together and forced them to relax. "Right now I can only keep three of them going. The rest will require a lot of work and materials."

"But how in the hell can you support the girls and yourself with only half your greenhouses in working order?"

She straightened her shoulders and tilted up her chin. "I can't."

Bain was silent for a moment as he gazed at her. "That's why you needed a tenant for the apartment," he said at last.

"The added income the apartment brings in will help fix up the other three greenhouses so I can expand the business."

He dropped the beet into her hand. "I see." He went back to scrubbing beets. "If you get the other three greenhouses up and operational, will you be able to support yourself and the girls?"

"Oh, yes." She finished her glass of champagne and started slicing again. "When I get all six operational, I'll be able to be more seasonal. Right now spring and summer are my big seasons. But with six going I can devote an entire greenhouse to poinsettias, one for chrysanthemums for fall, and another one for houseplants."

She went on to tell him about the other plants and flowers she wanted to include in her expanded business. It felt wonderful talking to someone about her plans and dreams. Bain didn't contribute a lot to the conversation besides an occasional question or two, but he seemed to understand.

Half the bottle of champagne was gone when she added the final spices and herbs to the mason jars full of beets and tightened down the lids. She placed the jars in the canner and set it on the rear burner of the stove. Turning to Bain, she smiled cheerfully. "So what do you think?"

Bain placed his empty glass on the drainboard. He couldn't tell if Erin was so happy because of the champagne or because all the beets were finally done. He slowly crossed the room to her and brushed back a wayward curl from her cheek. "I think you're a beautiful, intelligent, and strong woman."

"You do?"

The back of his fingers caressed the satiny smoothness of her cheek. "Not many women would have stayed here and built a dream for themselves. Why didn't you move back to the city? Your brother and parents are there. They could have helped you with the girls after your husband died."

She pressed her cheek into his palm. "My mother would tell you it's because I've never done anything the easy way, but that's not the reason. If I went back and accepted their help, it wouldn't have been my dream then. It would have been everybody's." She lightly cupped his jaw in her hand. "Didn't you ever have a dream of your own?"

Bain's expression hardened and he closed his eyes against the torment. *Oh, yes, I had a dream once.*

"Bain?" she whispered.

He opened his eyes and tried to smile. The past was past, and there was nothing he could do about it. "I had a dream once."

"Can't it come true?"

"There's a chance, but not the way I had always envisioned it."

She stared intently at him, obviously trying to understand. "Your writing?"

Bain held her gaze for a moment before lowering his. "Some dreams go beyond the scope of reason."

"Is your dream so unreasonable?"

"Some dreams change with time, Erin." He pulled her closer.

"Did yours?" She stroked his jaw with trembling fingers.

"I learned to dream from day to day, minute by minute."

Cupping his face, she forced his mouth closer to hers. "And what did you dream of today?"

"You." He captured her tormenting smile with a brief, hard kiss.

She smiled at him. "What about me?"

His mouth was hot and hungry as it skimmed down her neck and feasted on her shoulder. "I dreamed of laying you down at the edge of Lake Cayuga and making love to you until the waters all dried up and blew away into some pitiful little dust ball."

She shivered. "Was that before or after my swimming lesson?"

"During." Pulling her toward him, he leaned back against the refrigerator, scattering magnets and colorful drawings everywhere. He groaned as her lithe body pressed up against him. Molten lava burned the front of him as the cool metal of the refrigerator pressed against his back, bringing him back to reality.

"What are you dreaming about now?" She playfully nipped at his lower lip.

Bain closed his eyes and prayed for strength. Thank heavens his conscience was winning out. He wanted nothing more in life than to carry Erin upstairs to her bedroom and make love till dawn, but he couldn't. He couldn't chance taking the next step in their relationship without knowing why he was doing it. This was Erin he was holding in his arms, not some woman he wanted for only a one-night stand or even some month-long affair. This was the mother of his children, the woman who quite possibly was holding his dreams within her hands. Until he could better understand the various emotions rioting through his body and mind, he would have to slow down. Coming over here tonight bearing chilled champagne and hot kisses had been a mistake. A huge mistake, one that he was going to pay dearly for during the many nights to come. Why couldn't he simply enjoy Erin's company without wanting her?

Since he couldn't back up, he gently moved Erin back a step and slipped out from between her and the refrigerator. "Do you know what I would truly love?"

She tilted her head and looked at him. "What?"

"A piece of that peach pie from last night."

Erin's mouth fell open in disbelief. The man was kissing her senseless one minute and begging for food the next. "You want peach pie?"

"Only if you have an extra slice."

She shrugged and turned back to the refrigerator. "Sure, why not? It makes perfect sense to me." Her fingers trembled slightly as she wrapped them around the handle. The only picture left on the

white door was one Caitlin had drawn that evening
and had secured with a half-dozen plastic magnets
shaped like vegetables. It was a colorful rendition of
four stick people standing in the lake. A name was
printed in her childish letters under each figure:
"Mom," "Arlene," "Me," and the last name printed
with Caitlin's favorite color, red, was under the
biggest smiling figure, "Bain."

Maybe it had been a mistake renting out the
apartment to him, Erin thought as she stared at
the picture. Her daughters were becoming increas-
ingly attached to him, and the feelings he provoked
within her were unsettling, to say the least. Caitlin
was at that very impressionable age when she knew
other kids had a daddy and she didn't. What was she
going to do if Caitlin or Arlene got it into their
stubborn little heads that Bain would be the perfect
daddy? Bain was obviously trying to straighten out
his life and recuperate. Someone had dealt him a
severe blow, and not just to his leg. More than once
she'd felt he was hiding something, holding back a
vital piece of his person from her and the kids. Hell,
as far as she knew, he could be holding it back from
himself too. The healing process was a long and
twisted road. What Bain didn't need was an instant
family. No wonder he pulled back every time things
got a little heated up. What he needed was a friend,
not a lover.

She opened the refrigerator and pulled out the remaining peach pie covered in plastic wrap. "How about I warm this up and make some coffee?" She glanced over her shoulder and flashed a friendly smile. "There's an old Humphry Bogart movie on television tonight, if you care to watch it with me."

Bain jammed his hands into the pockets of his jeans and punched an imaginary brick wall in his mind. "Sure, why not?" He was, after all, the one who had called it quits just when it was getting interesting. So why did it irritate the hell out of him that Erin was taking it so well?

FIVE

Bain sat on a huge stack of peat-moss bags and listened to the laughter coming from inside one of the greenhouses. He felt like a poor orphan with his nose pressed up against the toy-store window the day before Christmas. So close, yet so far away.

The girls' high-pitched squeals of delight brought a smile to his face, but Erin's musical laughter caused it to slip back into a worried frown. What in the hell was he going to do with Erin? For the past week she had been treating him like a brother, and it was aggravating him no end. If he wanted a sister, he would go down to Virginia and visit Autumn and her growing tribe of Munchkins.

If he didn't want Erin for a sister, though, what did he want her for? A lover, a mother of his children, or how about a wife? How about all three? How was he supposed to separate any of them? She already was the mother of his children, and becoming lovers with her would be heaven, but the wife part threw him into a tailspin. He'd never contemplated taking a wife before. Sure, he'd always thought that one day he would give up undercover work, find Miss Right, and settle down to raise a passel of kids. He had been forced out of undercover work, and the passel of kids had been dwindled down to two little angels who didn't even know he was their father. As for Erin being Miss Right, that was anybody's guess. For days he had been trying to separate Erin the woman from Erin the mother, and couldn't.

He leaned farther back onto the bags and listened to the girls' hysterical rendition of "Old Mac-Donald" with Erin taking the lead. Caitlin made a marvelous cow, and Arlene could out-oink a pig, but Erin's "cluck cluck here, and a cluck cluck there" was as flat as a three-hour beer. He couldn't see exactly what was going on inside the greenhouse because most of the framework was covered with thick, foggy plastic. It was Erin's economical way of keeping her business operational.

He had given that straightforward, no-nonsense, anyway-you-can attitude to the fictional female detective he'd created a week earlier. After he'd first kissed Erin last Sunday night, he'd gone back to his apartment and had stayed up the entire night writing. He had found the perfect partner for his jaded police detective and hero, Shamus Mulligan. Her name was Fiona Muldoon. She had legs that went on forever and enough sass and spirit to make even Shamus stand up and howl. She was intelligent, strong-minded, and gorgeous. In the chapter he had finished late the night before, he had defied manly tradition and had had Fiona save Shamus's butt from being tossed off a seventeen-story apartment building. For the first time Shamus had looked beyond the cover-girl-perfect face of his partner and seen the steely determination of a police detective doing her job. Fiona had displayed amazing courage and steady hands, with just a hint of vulnerability causing her lower lip to quiver slightly. It was the same look Erin got during their daily swimming lessons. She was determined to show the girls how easy it was to swim while hiding her own fears. Bain was often tempted to kiss away that quiver, just as Shamus had been. Neither of them had given in to the temptation.

Caitlin dashed out of the greenhouse mooing like a deranged Holstein. "Bain, Bain!" she shouted as she ran over to him.

He smiled and patted the bag next to him. "Who let you out of the barn?"

Caitlin giggled and climbed up onto the bag. "Did you hear our song?"

"Yes, sweetheart. You make a wonderful cow."

The greenhouse door opened again, and Erin and Arlene came out. "But Arlene had better watch it that some farmer doesn't take her home to his pigpen."

Arlene scampered up onto his lap, smearing dirt and peat up his jeans and onto his shirt. "What about Mommy?"

Bain raised an eyebrow and glanced at Erin. She looked tired, hot, and sweaty. She had a streak of dirt smudged across her cheek, her hair was unraveling from its topknot, and her hands were filthy. She looked incredibly sexy and natural. "She makes nice horse sounds."

Arlene frowned and looked up at Bain. "Mommy was a chicken, not the horsey."

Bain saw a mulish gleam enter Erin's eyes. "Are you sure, Arlene? She sounded like a horse to me."

Erin stalked away from them, turning on the outside spigot and starting to wash off her arms and legs with the hose. Bain was pushing his luck by making fun of her animal sounds. There were two things she prided herself on doing well. One was getting Arlene's clothes clean every wash day and the other was knowing how to make animal sounds. To think that for days she had been extra nice to him. She had even gone as far as sending Caitlin and Arlene over to his apartment with leftover meat loaf and a plate full of sugar cookies the girls helped to bake. The man's gratitude was deplorable.

She kicked off her sneakers, angled the hose to her legs, and allowed the cool water to run in rivers down them. Working all morning in a greenhouse was like planting petunias in a sauna. She cupped a handful of water and poured it over the back of her neck.

"Mommy was a chicken," she heard Arlene declare.

"Your mommy's chicken," Bain answered, "sounded like it was run over by Old MacDonald's tractor."

Erin eyed the distance between her and Bain sitting there so smugly with Arlene on his lap for protection. She ignored her daughters' giggling and splashed some water onto her face.

When she was certain Bain thought he was safe, she whirled and turned the full force of the water right on him.

Caitlin's and Arlene's giggles turned to shouts of glee as the water bounced off Bain, showering them with a hail of water and floating peat particles. Bain quickly lowered Arlene to the ground and made a mad dash toward Erin.

Erin held her ground and tightened her grip on the hose. "Make fun of my clucking, will you?" She aimed the water right at his chest. Water not only soaked him, but it continued to splash in every direction, coating her, the girls, and the ground.

Bain's feet started to slip and slide out from under him. He nearly lost his balance twice, but managed to make it through the puddles and latch on to the gushing hose. "Now you did it!"

Erin smiled determinedly and held on to the only weapon at her disposal. With a mighty yank she tried to dislodge his grip, only to have her own feet slip out from under her. In a blinding instant of confusion, arms and legs tangled together, and both Erin and Bain hit the soaked ground with a resounding splat.

Mud splashed everywhere. The girls stared in amazement at their mother lying on the ground laughing.

"Are you all right?" Bain asked, staring down at her sprawled beneath him. He maneuvered his body so his elbows took most of his weight.

The gushing hose was trapped between their bodies. Erin laughed as water squirted up and pelted his chin. "I'm fine." Her laughter turned to a shriek as Bain angled his chin and the water ricocheted off him and into her face. "I feel like some fountain that tourists are always throwing pennies in and making wishes."

Bain's chuckle caused the water to shoot off in a different direction. He brushed a mud-soaked curl away from her face and moved the hose out from between their bodies. "Did I ever tell you how wonderful you look in mud?" Her eyes were shining with happiness, and her tempting smile was begging to be tasted.

"I get that compliment a lot." She reached up to brush a speck of mud off his cheek and ended up smearing on more.

Bain shivered as the warmth of her fingers penetrated his cool skin. He captured her hand and glanced at it. It was covered in mud. "I take it my face looks about as good as your hand."

She bit her lip to keep from laughing. "I missed a spot here," she said. Reaching up with her other hand, she smeared another streak down the other side of his face.

A low, playful growl vibrated in the back of his throat. His fingers toyed with the still-running hose. "So you want to play?"

Before Erin could reply, Arlene jumped into the growing puddle surrounding them and shouted, "Mud pies!"

Bain and Erin both instinctively turned away from the splashing mud and water and yelled, "Arlene, no!"

"Me play too," Arlene demanded as she stomped her foot for emphasis.

Bain rolled off Erin and started to squirt Arlene's legs with the hose. "So you want to play too?"

Arlene giggled and splashed some more. Erin sat up and grabbed the hose. With a triumphant yell she turned it on Bain again. Caitlin took one look at the laughing, mud-covered adults and jumped right in.

Erin found herself being wrestled, tickled, and smeared with mud. Water and mud flew everywhere and coated everything. Shouts, childish animal noises, and laughter filled the air. She and the girls tried desperately to best Bain. They ganged up on him during the attacks, only to lose ground when he grabbed one of the girls and started tickling unmercifully. Little arms and legs wiggled in every direction, and high-pitched squeals threatened to pierce their eardrums.

Erin rolled over trying to protect Arlene from being tickled and reached for the hose Bain had gotten away from her. She felt strong arms encircle her waist and flip her over onto her back. Cool mud squished out beneath her. Bain pressed his body onto the lower squirming portion of hers. His groan had nothing to do with pain and everything to do with desire as she tried to buck him off.

"Mommy, Mommy, we'll save you," Arlene cried.

Caitlin jumped on Bain's back, causing Erin to be pressed deeper into the mud. "Let my mommy go," she demanded.

Erin laughed as both of her daughters tore into Bain like crazed terriers after a bone.

Bain was laughing so hard, he nearly lost his grip on Erin's slippery wrists. He anchored them on either side of her head. "Call off your attack squad."

"Never!" She glanced at her daughters and winked. "Is this the part where I give you my name, rank, and Social Security number?"

Caitlin and Arlene picked up the discarded hose and aimed it at Bain's back.

He secured both of Erin's wrists with one hand and started to tickle her. "Say uncle."

Erin laughed while trying to move away from his tickling fingers. "Never."

His fingers danced over her rib cage. "Say uncle."

She couldn't take it any longer. Tickling had to be one of the worst forms of torture. In between laughs she gulped for air and whispered, "Uncle."

"I can't hear you." He stared down at her, his fingers stilling against her rapidly rising and falling rib cage.

Erin caught her breath at Bain's expression. She knew her daughters were still spraying water and tugging on his shirt, but he didn't seem to notice them. His warm fingers inched higher, and his mouth started to descend. She saw the kiss coming, looked at her daughters, and said, "Uncle."

Bain glanced over his shoulder at the curious duo staring back at him and groaned. He let go of Erin and rolled onto his back. "I won."

She released the breath she had been holding and relaxed. A chuckle escaped her as she noticed her daughters' disappointed expressions. "Don't worry, girls, we'll get him the next time."

Both girls grinned. The chance to frolic in the mud again was too good to ignore. "Tomorrow?" Caitlin asked.

"No, not tomorrow," Erin said in alarm. She should have known she was going to have a hard time with the girls. She was constantly pleading with them not to get dirty. A couple weeks of Bain's influence and not only were they playing in the mud, so was she. Embarrassed at being caught at such unmotherly conduct, she said, "Why don't you two take that hose and water Mommy's plants around the house?"

Caitlin and Arlene started to fight over the hose. "Me do! Me do!"

Erin frowned at her daughters. "I said together." Both girls glanced at her, then each of them placed one hand on the hose and started to drag it around the corner of the house. "Caitlin, Arlene?" They stopped and turned around. "While you're at it, try to wash some of that mud off yourselves."

Bain watched the two little tykes disappear around

the corner, then he sat up and studied Erin. "We have a problem."

"We do?" She could think of quite a few problems they had. Like how much she had wanted that kiss.

"Yeah." He stood up and held out a hand.

Erin grabbed it and allowed him to pull her up. They were both covered in mud. She grimaced as she pulled her soaking T-shirt away from her body. "Gross" didn't begin to describe how it felt. "What is our problem?"

His gaze fixed on her body as she released the T-shirt. It was plastered back to her chest within an instant. He roughly cleared his throat. "I want to kiss you."

She looked up, startled. That was the last thing she had thought he would say. She was standing there covered with mud from head to toe and he wanted to kiss her. Was he insane? Her gaze traveled from the top of his wet hair, over his dirt-smeared face, past his mud-coated shirt and jeans. There wasn't a clean spot on him. Her grin was spontaneous. "So what's the problem?"

He laughed and hauled her into his arms. His mouth was hot and hungry as it found hers.

Her arms encircled his neck and forced him closer. Delicious sensations warmed her stomach as he pulled back and gazed down at her. "Would you have a problem if I do that more often?"

She stared dreamily at him. "No."

"Good." He grinned and handed her his wallet.

She stared at it, frowning as a small pile of pocket change joined it. "What are you doing?"

He kicked off his sneakers and started to walk toward the lake. "Taking a daytime version of a cold shower."

"Why?"

He stopped, looked back at her, and shook his head. "If you have to ask, Erin, we definitely do have a problem."

She watched as he walked straight into the lake. When he was waist deep, he went under. Surfacing several yards farther out, he started to swim. A silly, warm grin spread across her face as she watched his powerful strokes. Lord, how she'd missed his kisses.

"Arlene, honey, you're supposed to hand me the can of putty when I ask for it, not poke your fingers into it." Bain held the pane of glass in place with one hand and tried to grab the can with his other hand. His arm was a good twelve inches too short. "Could you hand me the can now, Arlene?"

Arlene looked up at him standing on the ladder and grinned. She pulled out her fingers. "Got ya'."

Gray sticky ooze coated two fingers. She handed the can to him and wiped her fingers down the front of her once-clean green-and-white-striped top.

Bain grimaced as he took the sticky can. Why had he ever told Erin he would watch Arlene so she and Caitlin could go back-to-school shopping? He glanced at Arlene's dirt-covered smiling face and chuckled. The saints really had to have been on vacation the day she was born. The thought of having all three of his favorite ladies out of his sight for hours had caused his mouth to open before his brain had kicked in. Watching Arlene was like trying to rope a tornado. The child had more energy than six twisters and was known to be more destructive. "Thank you, honey. You can go back to playing with your pots now."

"Got ya'." Arlene sat back down in the center aisle of the greenhouse and continued to build her towering stacks using dozens of green plastic potting pots.

Bain shook his head and went back to work. For the past two weeks, in exchange for lunch and dinner, he had been working three hours every afternoon repairing the three greenhouses Erin already had up and running. It was the perfect solution. Erin was stubborn enough not to accept his free labor, and he was greedy for every minute he could spend with the girls and her. His days consisted of writing four hours every morning, working on the green-houses, and swimming lessons. His nights were spent with Erin, either watching some old-time movie or rocking on the porch, talking and kissing. Bain considered himself one of the luckiest men in the world. Frustrated as hell, but lucky.

He was reaching for his measuring tape to measure the next opening that needed new glass, when Caitlin's voice penetrated the greenhouse. "Bain! Arlene!" He shuddered as the screen door to the first greenhouse slammed shut. "Bain, where are you?"

"In here, Cait! In here!" Arlene yelled. A towering stack of green pots went flying as Arlene raced to the screen door.

Bain shook his head to clear his hearing. There was absolutely nothing wrong with Arlene's lungs. He could hear the gravel crunching under Caitlin's feet as she ran to the right greenhouse. The crinkling of plastic bags as they slapped against her legs confirmed his suspicion that the shopping trip had been a success.

Caitlin's yank on the screen door nearly unhinged it. "Bain! Arlene! Wait until you see what I got. *Two* new dresses!" She bounded into the greenhouse with the unlimited energy only a child could possess.

"Caitlin Allison Flynn, don't you dare open those packages in the greenhouse," Erin yelled.

Bain chuckled as Erin came dashing in on Caitlin's heels. She looked exhausted, windblown, and entirely kissable. He wanted to pull her into his arms and crush those tempting lips beneath his. Lord, how he had missed her, and she had only gone shopping. He didn't like, but he respected, the distance Erin kept between them when the girls were around.

"I see that the mighty shoppers have returned," he said as he descended the ladder. He made a quick grab and saved one of the bags Caitlin was holding from being dumped on the gravel floor. He handed the bag to Erin and tenderly stroked the inside of her wrist. "By the look of things I'd say the economy just got a boost."

"I couldn't seem to stop myself."

Desire heated his body. Everything she said seemed provocative. "From what?"

"Buying her both dresses. I couldn't make up my mind which one to buy. She looked adorable in both."

"There's nothing wrong with that." His fingers stroked up her arm. "She's just like her mother, looks adorable in anything."

Heat flushed her cheeks as goosebumps broke

out across her arm. "She's my first baby to go to nursery school."

He stepped closer and teased the sleeve of her blouse with his fingers. "I understand completely."

Erin's gaze never left his lips. "You do?"

He sucked in a harsh breath. He had no idea what they were talking about, but whatever it was, it had nothing to do with what they were thinking. Erin wanted his mouth. He saw it in the darkening of her eyes and the flush sweeping up her cheeks. He gripped her arm and pulled her closer. The hell with her reserve around the girls. It was about time they saw their mother get kissed, because he planned on doing a lot more of it in the future.

"Me see. Me see." Arlene wedged herself between the two adults and tried to look into the bags.

Erin came out of her daze in a hurry. Bain had been about to kiss her. His intentions had been clearly declared by the heat in his gaze. She looked down at Arlene's head as she tried to bury her face into one of the bags. One little kiss in front of the girls surely wouldn't hurt. She lifted herself onto her toes and quickly kissed his mouth. "Are you almost finished in here?"

Bain seemed too surprised to answer for a moment. "I have a couple more cracked panes of glass to replace, and the door needs some work before it's as good as new."

Erin looked around the greenhouse with pride. Almost all of the plastic she had jimmie rigged to hold out the weather these last two years had been replaced with sparkling new glass. New gravel coated the floor, and Bain had worked wonders on the drainage system for all three greenhouses. Rows of freshly painted tables overflowed with flowering plants, tiny shoots, and the green foliage of house-plants. In a matter of days she would be able to concentrate on repairing the first empty greenhouse and fulfilling her dreams. She couldn't have done it without him. "Have I thanked you lately for the wonderful job you're doing?"

"Every time I sit down to one of your meals, you do."

She blushed. "No, I mean really thank you. They look wonderful, Bain." She moved the bag farther away from Arlene's sticky fingers.

"It's been my pleasure." Bain noticed the determined look on Arlene's face and picked her up before she did something drastic. "I think someone here is getting impatient to see what's in all these bags."

Erin shifted her attention back to the girls. "Go wash up and I'll get out some cookies and something cold to drink. Caitlin, you can show Arlene and Bain what you got after a snack."

Bain quickly lowered his squirming bundle to her

feet. By the way both girls dashed out of the greenhouse and ran toward the house, someone might have thought Santa had come early. He pulled Erin closer and brushed her mouth with his. "Now it's my turn to thank you."

"For what?"

"Trust." *An honor I don't deserve.*

"Trust?"

"Today was the first time you ever left Arlene with anyone, wasn't it?"

"Well, yes." She shifted the bag nervously in her hand.

"Today was also the first time you ever kissed a man in front of your children, wasn't it?"

A blush stole up her cheek. "So?"

"So!" He pulled her closer for a long, slow kiss. Emotions clogged his throat, and a sheen of extra moisture coated his eyes. "Thank you for sharing your life with me."

The plastic bag banged against his back as her arms encircled his neck. "You're welcome," she said, but she was frowning slightly.

He playfully nipped at her lower lip. "Do you remember what happened the last time you sent Arlene to the house to wash up?"

The color drained from her face, and she dashed out of the greenhouse.

Bain breathed a sigh of relief as Erin ran across

the yard and into the house. She had picked up on his emotions. She had known something wasn't right. He glanced around the sun-drenched greenhouse and frowned. Erin and the girls were surrounded by colors, a kaleidoscope of happiness. He wanted to stay in their world and bask in their sunshine. How could he do that? The truth was a heavy, dark cloud he carried around, threatening to rain on everyone's parade.

He didn't deserve Erin's trust. He didn't deserve the growing embers of love that sometimes brightened her eyes. How in the hell could he tell Erin the truth? With a heavy heart he started to walk toward the house. How in the hell could he not?

Bain softly closed the screen door behind him and crossed the kitchen floor. Erin was standing at the sink with her back toward him. He snuck up behind her and kissed her neck.

She sighed, tilted her head to give him a better angle, and dropped the vegetable brush she had been using to scrub the sinkful of carrots.

He brushed her braid out of his way and nibbled his way up her neck to the sensitive spot behind her ear. "Are the girls in bed?"

"Hmmm. . . ." She reached for a towel and dried her hands. "You missed them by an hour."

"Sorry." He nipped at her earlobe. "I started working on the book and lost track of time."

She turned and leaned against the sink. "That's okay, I understand." His mouth brushed her cheek. "When are you going to let me read it?"

He raised his head and gazed down at her. "Are you serious?"

She frowned. "Of course I'm serious. Why wouldn't I want to read your book?"

"I never thought about allowing anyone to read it."

"How are you planning on getting it published if no one reads it?"

He shifted his weight and avoided looking at her. "I wasn't meaning the publishers."

"You don't want me to read it, do you?" she asked, hurt. For weeks she'd thought their relationship had been growing. Their nightly kisses had turned from heated ecstasy to pure torture. She wanted to go forward with their relationship, and he didn't want her to share in his personal accomplishment.

He gently cupped her cheek. "It's not that, Erin."

"Then, what is it?"

"What if you don't like it?"

She heard the vulnerability and uncertainty in his voice and threw herself into his arms. "Oh, Bain. Did you write it?"

"Of course I wrote it." He hugged her closer and breathed in the fresh, flowery scent of her shampoo.

"Then I'm going to love it." She brushed a string of kisses down his jaw.

"How can you be so sure?"

"Because"—she captured his face between her hands—"you wrote it." She rose up and devoured his mouth with a kiss that was guaranteed to knock his writing stride off for the rest of the night.

Bain came out of the kiss dazed and aroused. "I think you might be a little prejudiced."

She playfully toyed with his hair. "Just a little."

"Wait till I get a couple more chapters done, and then I'll let you read it."

"Really?"

"Really." He chuckled and captured her playful fingers before they could cause any more damage to his galloping hormones. Saying good night to Erin every night was the hardest thing he had ever done. And each night it was becoming harder. "It's getting late." He stroked her lower lip with his thumb. "I should be heading back."

Erin gathered up every ounce of boldness she possessed and said, "Stay."

He stared at her. "Stay what?"

"Stay the night."

SIX

Bain carried Erin into the bedroom and slowly lowered her feet to the floor. He stopped her hand as she reached for the light switch. "Leave it off."

Her gaze slid to his leg, and she smiled gently. "I won't mind."

He closed the door and pulled her back into his arms. "But I would." His fingers tugged off the rubber band holding the end of her braid. Silken waves unraveled themselves and wrapped around his fingers. "I want everything to be perfect tonight."

She pulled his head down to hers. Her breath sweetly tantalized his lips. "It already is."

A heavy groan filled the room as he surrendered to her bidding. His fingers found the row of buttons running down the bodice of her dress. Without breaking the heated kiss he released every one of those buttons.

Erin's fingers shook with need as she unbuttoned his shirt and pushed it off his shoulders. A sigh of delight escaped her as he helped shrug the shirt off. Her hands raced up and down his back, memorizing every detail, every muscle, every contour.

He broke the kiss and nuzzled her face. "Lord, how I want you, Erin."

She smiled at the way he said her name, all breathless and shaky. Arching her back, she felt her dress slide off her shoulders to land in a puddle of cotton at her feet. "I want you too." She wiggled her toes and slipped out of her white leather sandals.

Bain raised his mouth from her slender neck. The only light penetrating the darkness came in from the windows overlooking the lake. The moon was full and bright, but it still left most of the room in deep shadows. In the dimness he tried to read her expression but failed. "Say my name, Erin." He brushed her mouth with a hungry kiss. "I need to hear you say my name."

She understood his need. There was no room in her bedroom for third parties. Without the benefit of light he couldn't see if she was really with him or some distant ghost from her past. She kissed his cheek, whispering, "Bain." She lightly bit his chin as her hands pulled him closer. "Bain." She stood on her toes and captured his lower lip between her teeth. Her fingers shook as she undid his belt and unsnapped the fastening of his jeans. "I want you, Bain."

He groaned and buried his face into her silky hair. "Thank you."

Her hands stilled in surprise. "For what?"

"For being you, Erin. For just being you." He released the clasp of her bra and gently brushed the straps down her slender arms. The scrap of silky lace landed somewhere at their feet. His hands stroked her stomach, then swept up to cradle the sweet fullness of her breasts. Perfection overflowed in his hands.

Erin gasped for breath as desire tightened her stomach and caused her breasts to swell. Her nipples peaked further as Bain's thumbs stroked them into hard pebbles of sensation. The lighter his touch, the more she felt. Her hands clutched at his hips, trying to bring him closer. She wanted more.

Bain lowered his head and tenderly circled each protruding nub with the tip of his tongue. He shuddered as Erin stroked his rigid manhood through his pants. When a fingernail lightly ran down the metal teeth of his zipper, he quickly grabbed her hand. Lifting it to his lips, he kissed each fingertip as he reached over and yanked the covers down on the bed.

Erin felt herself being gently lowered to the bed. She listened and tried to watch Bain finish undressing. The darkness prevented her seeing anything except the slightest outline. She hated the darkness. It reminded her of secrets and shamefulness. Bain's injury must really be awful if he was embarrassed to turn on the lights. Or was he afraid she would reject him? Did she seem that shallow in his eyes?

As he started to lower himself onto the bed, she encircled his neck with her arms and hung on tight. Her mouth greedily sought his. She wanted to show him there was nothing shameful in two people making love and that the human body was beautiful, no matter what condition it was in. He might feel more comfortable hiding in the dark, but she didn't. She wanted to see Bain. She wanted to see the man who had slipped into her heart when she hadn't even been looking. The next time they made love, it would be with the lights on.

Bain responded to her feverish kisses with fire. His heart and soul answered every one of her demanding assaults with a passion that was new to him. She was a wildcat commanding more, and he gave it. Never before had the intensity of such raw passion and desire driven him. Within an instant he had removed the last silken barrier between them and was poised above her. He forced his mouth away from hers. His fingers trembled as they brushed a curl away from her cheek. "Are you ready, Erin?"

She captured his hand and drew it down her

body. It slid over her rapidly pounding heart, pressed against her quivering abdomen, and tunneled through the thatch of curls guarding her womanhood.

Bain groaned and buried his mouth against her neck as his fingers found the dewiness between her thighs. She was moist, ready, and his. His finger slipped into the center of the moisture and he was rewarded with a purr of pure pleasure.

Erin arched her hips against his hand. "Does that answer your question?"

He removed his finger and settled his hips more firmly between her thighs. His control was splintered into a million fragments of good intentions. The time for questions had passed. With mind-shattering swiftness he entered her heat and started their fervent journey.

The rhythm he set rapidly quickened to a wild frenzy of clinging arms and straining bodies. Both tried to reach the crest, both tried to hold back and wait for the other. In a mad climax that bordered on savage they both peaked within milliseconds of each other. Bain was positive Erin called his name first, and she was certain he had shouted hers into the depths of the pillow cradling her head.

Erin stared up into the darkness and lovingly ran her fingers through Bain's hair. His breathing was still rapid against her breasts, and she marveled again at the strength of the human heart. Hers should have burst. Possibly from the love, or the joy, but most assuredly from the strain. Emotions she had never known existed were assaulting her from every angle.

Could a person fall in love so quickly? She'd never believed in love at first sight, or even second sight. To her way of thinking, love took time and nurturing to bloom. Just like one of her flowers. It started with a tiny seed, and given plenty of water, sunlight, and rich soil, it would start to grow. If the nurturing continued and all the elements stayed true, one day it would reach its full potential and blossom. So if it wasn't love she was feeling, what was it?

It wasn't just sex. Any female and male could have sex. There was no way she could experience what she had just shared with Bain with anyone else. It had been special. Unique. Hell, who was she kidding? It had been so hot, the sheets were probably singed. A fiery blush swept up her cheeks as she recalled their frantic lovemaking.

Her arms tightened around Bain as he tried to move. "No, don't."

He nuzzled her breast. "I'm too heavy for you." His hand stroked her thigh as he shifted his weight off her.

She relaxed as he settled beside her and pulled her into his arms. For a minute there she'd thought he was going to leave. She needed to hang on to his warmth. Her world was rapidly spinning out of control, and she needed someone to hold, if only for the night.

Silence and contentment filled the room. Bain managed to pull the sheet over their bodies as a cool evening breeze blew in through the opened windows.

"Bain?" Erin's voice was thick with sleep.

His arms tightened their hold, but he didn't open his eyes. "Hmmm. . . ."

"Thank you." She snuggled deeper into his warmth and fell asleep listening to the steady beat of his heart.

"It was entirely my pleasure," he whispered, and followed her into an exhausted slumber.

Bain slowly came awake with two thoughts drifting through his mind. One, it was daylight, and two, someone was planting light kisses down his chest. The grin spreading across his face was quickly replaced with a scowl as he tried to yank the covers up.

Erin held on to the sheet and continued her sensual assault on Bain's chest. She wove her fingers through the auburn curls and kissed a rippling muscle.

He clenched his stomach muscles harder and glared at the window. It wasn't light out! Daybreak hadn't broken yet. Erin had switched on the lights. He tried to grab the blanket that was lowering still farther down his hips. "Erin, stop."

She raised her head and gazed at him. "Why?"

"You know why." The scars were red and ugly. He wouldn't be able to stand to see Erin's loving gaze turn to revulsion. He had found his dream earlier in her arms and couldn't chance losing her.

Her chin rose a notch. "You think I'm that shallow?"

"I don't think you're shallow at all." Still he held on to the blanket.

She placed a whisper-soft kiss on the intriguing indentation of his navel. "Then what are you afraid of?"

He groaned as desire rocketed through him and made a ten-point landing all in one area. The thin summer blanket did little to disguise his arousal. "Turn off the light," he growled, "and I'll show you who's afraid."

Her laughter teased the coarse curls bordering the edge of the blanket. "I thought cops were supposed to be rough and tough."

"We are. . . . I am." He swallowed hard as her hand passed over the blanket. A cold sweat broke out across his brow. "I mean I was."

"Chicken? Bain."

His gaze grew serious. "About certain things, yes."

Her fingers lightly caressed the back of his hand clutching the blanket. "I'll make a deal with you."

She pried a finger away from the blanket. "If for any reason I get upset with what I find, we'll turn off the light and do it your way." Another finger released its death grip. "But if I find what I think I'll find, the light stays on." One more finger disengaged itself as she placed a light kiss on his hip.

Bain held his breath as the blanket was slowly lowered.

Half an hour later Erin smiled and placed a string of wanton kisses across Bain's chest and neck until she encountered a pair of hungry lips. Within a heartbeat she found herself being rolled over and pressed into the mattress by Bain's weight. Her laughter was muffled by his demanding mouth.

He raised his head and tried to catch his breath. "Are you trying to kill me, woman?"

She wiggled enticingly and scraped her fingernails down his back. "Are you complaining?" She felt womanly, seductive, and entirely ravished. Who would have thought it could be like this?

He captured a semihard nipple between his lips and brought it to perfection. He grinned down at his handiwork. "Never!"

She stiffened as his mouth sought the other nipple. "Bain?"

He quickly glanced up at the sound of distress in her voice. "What's wrong?"

Her anxious gaze darted from his eyes to their bodies. "I . . ." She tried to squirm out from under him. "I mean, we . . ." She glanced around the room, looking for the right words. "I mean, you didn't . . ."

"I didn't what?"

"Use anything."

"Use anything?"

"You know." She blushed and looked away. "Birth control."

Bain groaned, rolling over onto his back and throwing his forearm over his eyes. For a minute there she had scared the hell out of him. "You don't have to worry, Erin."

She pulled the sheet up to cover her nakedness. "I don't?"

"No." He raised his arm and glanced at her. She looked all sexy and warm with her hair wild and her lips red and swollen from his kisses. She deserved the whole truth. She'd once told him that honesty was the foundation of any great relationship. He wasn't sure where their relationship was heading, but he knew she deserved that much from him. Pain tore at his heart as he said aloud for the first time, "I can't father a child." Erin seemed like the eternal earth mother. Maybe she wouldn't want a relationship with a man who couldn't give her any more children. Maybe the first part of the truth would end their relationship and he wouldn't have to tell her he had been the sperm donor for the girls.

Her curious gaze shot to his thigh. The scars were now hidden by the sheet she had pulled up. "Because of your accident?"

"It wasn't an accident, Erin."

He held her startled gaze for a full minute before she quietly said, "Tell me what happened."

Bain sighed in defeat. He didn't want to tell her the gruesome story, but he needed to tell her the truth. In a low, steady voice he explained what he used to do for the NYPD. He told her about drugs, about undercover cops and the price they sometimes had to pay. His voice trembled only slightly as he told her about the price he had paid. The price he would keep on paying for the rest of his life.

Erin listened with tear-filled eyes. When Bain had finished his story, she pulled him into her arms and rocked him. She was at a total loss for words.

The furious pounding of his heart slowed to a brisk gallop. He snuggled deeper under the covers and pulled her closer.

"Bain?"

"Hmmm?"

"I don't mean for this to sound this way, after all you've been through, but I'm glad you can't father any children."

Confused, he glanced up. "Why?"

"Because I allowed passion to overrule my common sense, not once but twice tonight."

"And an unplanned pregnancy was not on your New Year's Resolutions list this year, right?"

"Planned or unplanned, it wouldn't make a difference. I definitely should not, that's with a capital N-O-T, become pregnant."

"Why?" He moved away from her to study her face. "Did something go wrong when you carried the girls?"

She chuckled. "Bain, nothing, and I do mean nothing, went right when I carried the girls. I did not glow, I did not blossom, and I most certainly did not radiate. The highlight of carrying Caitlin for nine agonizing months was thirty-six hours of hard labor, and Arlene was worse."

Bain swallowed hard. Years of listening to his sisters-in-law joke about swollen ankles and the occasional lost breakfast hadn't prepared him for this. "Worse?"

"Let's just say because of my medical problems they couldn't take her cesarean, and I had to deliver her naturally."

"What's wrong with that?"

"She was a breech birth."

He paled. "After everything you went through with Caitlin, why did you have Arlene?"

"Because in my heart and soul I would have a

dozen children. It's my body that can't. Everything in my system goes completely haywire for nine months. The doctors say I shouldn't chance another pregnancy."

Bain heard the tears in her voice and pulled her into his embrace. Lord, what she must have gone through to have the girls. His girls. Now was the time for the rest of the truth. If he didn't tell her now, he might never find the courage again. He reluctantly released her and sat up on the side of the bed. "There's more I have to tell you."

She pulled up the covers and leaned back against the headboard. "About what?"

He stood up, slipped on his jeans, and started to pace. "Before my 'little accident' I was a perfectly normal male."

She tilted her head and examined his body. "You seem perfectly normal to me now."

"What I mean is I never used to be sterile." He stopped in front of her and groaned. She looked so warm and sexy with her hair all tangled and the flowered sheet barely covering her exquisite breasts. He took a deep breath and said a silent prayer. "Over five years ago I was in my family doctor's office for a routine checkup and he asked me a favor."

Erin held his anxious gaze and waited.

"Since I was totally healthy, young, and of sound mind, he asked me to donate some sperm so that a nice couple he knew could have a baby." He watched the color drain from Erin's cheeks. "I did. Over three years ago Dr. Shamus O'Donnell asked if I would donate another 'sample' so that the same nice couple could have a second child." Bain felt his stomach clench as Erin's expression turned horrified at the mention of Shamus O'Donnell's name. "I did."

Erin had to swallow three times before she could work up enough nerve to open her mouth. "You're Caitlin and Arlene's biological father, aren't you?"

"Yes."

She silently studied every slant, every line on his face. The resemblance had been there the whole time, only she'd never bothered to notice. Caitlin had his coloring, and neither one of them burned in the sun. He'd even told Caitlin she looked just like his mother. Why hadn't she seen the similarities? She looked up into his green eyes and asked, "Why?"

He shifted his weight uneasily. "I was young and healthy. I had my whole life in front of me. Why shouldn't I have helped out?"

"No, I mean why did you come here?" Fear clawed at her stomach as she clutched the sheet tighter. *Do sperm donors have any legal rights to their offspring?*

He obviously saw her fear and quickly tried to reassure her. "No, Erin don't even think it. The girls are one hundred percent yours. I wouldn't dream of coming between you." He started to pace the room again. "I came here for only one reason. I wanted to see what my children might have looked like. Don't you remember, I asked to speak to your husband? As far as I knew, the Flynns were still the nice young couple Doc O'Donnell had told me about."

"How did you know about the apartment?"

"I didn't know until you told me. I showed up here with a newspaper advertisement for an antique pie safe."

"I wasn't selling any pie safe."

"I know. The address was different, but it was the closest I could find. I figured I'd play the role of some dumb tourist, see the kids, and be on my way."

"To where?"

"North Dakota. I had a deputy job all lined up there."

She looked at him in complete bafflement. "So why did you stay?"

He stopped his pacing. "Honestly?"

"Isn't that what this whole thing is about?"

"Initially I stayed because of the girls. You offered me a golden opportunity to be near them. To be part of their life, if only for a little while."

"What about the job in North Dakota?"

"I turned it down a few days after I got here. I

realized that my life was heading in a different direction."

"Caitlin and Arlene's direction?"

"There was that, but I also realized how much you were coming to mean to me. I stayed because of you, Erin."

She frowned. "So what do we do now?"

He sat back down on the edge of the bed and ran his fingers through his hair. "That's just it, I don't know." He glanced at her and cracked a small smile. "I've never felt this way about another woman, Erin."

She answered his smile with a small one of her own. "There seems to be a lot of that going around lately." Maybe what they needed was time, she thought. Time for her to adjust to the fact that Bain was the girls' biological father and time to figure out where their relationship was heading.

He grinned at her. "You won't mind taking it slow and easy for a while so we both can adjust to this complicated situation?"

She glanced down at the thin sheet covering her naked body. The bed looked as if tag-team wrestlers had been practicing on it, and Bain was only wearing a pair of faded jeans. "Is this your idea of slow and easy?"

He caught the laughter dancing in her eyes and chuckled. Everything was going to work out. He had shaken their foundation and it had stood firm.

His fingers playfully teased the sheet covering her. "Hell, Erin, I haven't even hit slow and easy yet."

Her smile was pure rapture as he slowly pulled the sheet away.

Three weeks later Erin held her breath as Arlene took another step deeper into the lake. The cool water was over her dimpled knees and gently lapping at her thighs, and still she took another step toward Bain.

"That's a good girl, honey." Bain opened up his arms and grinned. "Two more steps and you made it."

Arlene glanced back at her mother and Caitlin standing at the water's edge and mustered up a brave smile. She turned back toward Bain and eyed the distance still between them. "Two?"

Bain squatted more. "Just two more, Arlene." The water barely reached his waist and the muscles in his thigh were screaming for relief, but he wasn't budging. They were at the critical stage of Arlene's swimming lessons. Either she was going to trust him or she wasn't.

Arlene slowly took a step nearer. She realized she was only one more step away from him and threw herself into his arms.

He held tight to his slippery bundle, trying to

steady himself. The weight of her body being propelled against his chest had nearly sent him over backward. Both of them would have tumbled into the water, not only causing a huge splash but flushing over a month's worth of swimming lessons down the tube. He found his balance and stood up, swinging the beaming Arlene in circles. "You did it!"

Erin and Caitlin rushed into the water and joined in the celebration. Arlene had voluntarily waded into water that came up to her chest. "You did it, sweetheart!" Erin exclaimed.

Bain scooped up Caitlin, too, and frolicked around in the water with them, sending up huge splashes and waves. His booming laughter drowned out the squeals from the girls clinging to his neck. Arlene had trusted him. His baby girl had trusted him to be there for her. He spun the girls one more time, just to hear their squeals, then faced Erin, basking in her radiant smile. "This calls for a celebration."

Erin's expression turned thoughtful. They looked so much like a family, she mused. Bain's resemblance to the two red-haired girls wiggling in his arms was remarkable. Anyone seeing them like this would automatically assume he was their father. And Bain had all the makings of a wonderful father.

He hoisted Caitlin up higher. "If you promise to try the lesson I was teaching you yesterday, I'll treat you all to dinner and a movie."

Both girls' eyes widened as they quickly turned toward their mother. "Can we, please?" Caitlin begged.

Erin came out of her daze. "What?"

Bain chuckled as Caitlin sighed in exasperation. "You haven't started dinner or anything, have you?" he asked.

"No, why?"

"Then it's my treat tonight. We'll dine on greasy fast food, pig out on buttery popcorn at the movies, and on the way home we'll stop at the ice-cream stand and order huge banana splits."

Erin looked at her daughters and sighed. Their mouths were hanging open and their eyes were as large as saucers. They never would have dreamed of doing all their favorite things in one night. The whole evening sounded nauseating to her, but then again the meat loaf and mashed potatoes she had planned was having the same effect. She lovingly tugged on Caitlin's ponytail and took her from Bain's arms. "I'm not sure what will suffer the most damage, our digestive systems or your wallet."

Both girls gave a loud cheer.

Bain swung Arlene up into the air. "Caitlin gets to pick the place to eat, and you get to pick the movie."

Arlene threw her arms around Bain's neck and

planted a sloppy kiss on his cheek. "I love you, Bain."

The color drained out of his face, and his balance wobbled for a second. *My daughter loves me!* She'd given him his first wet and sloppy kiss and she had blurted out those three magical words. His heart was beating wildly, and he suddenly felt like a daddy. His arms tightened around his precious burden as he laid his cheek against her damp baby curls. "The feeling's mutual, kid."

Heat surfaced in his face when he glanced up and noticed Erin's peculiar expression. He tried to make light of his intense reaction to Arlene's words by shrugging and saying, "What can I say, she's wrapped me around her little finger."

Erin continued to gaze curiously at Bain and Arlene. "She does that to a lot of people." For the first time she realized just how important Caitlin and Arlene were to Bain. They weren't simply some product from a sample he'd given at the doctor's office. They were the only children he would ever produce. His bloodline stopped with them. A small seed of doubt entered her mind. Just how far was Bain willing to go to be part of his children's lives?

"She must have inherited it from some other female I know," he said, smiling.

"Like who?"

He set Arlene down, and the girl ran to Caitlin at

the edge of the lake to discuss the night's activities. "Some red-headed witch who wrapped me around her finger the first minute I laid eyes on her."

Erin bit the inside of her cheek to keep from smiling. Her thoughts were way off center. Bain couldn't possibly make such exquisite love to her night after night just to keep the contact with his daughters. After all, he didn't have to tell her about being the sperm donor. She never would have known otherwise. She trailed the tips of her fingers across the top of the water. One eyebrow arched questioningly. "The first minute?"

He took a step closer and captured her hand. Bringing it up to his mouth, he placed a tender kiss on the first finger. "It was the way the breeze was teasing your hair." His lips brushed the next finger. "Did I ever tell you that you have the softest green eyes I have ever seen?" She shook her head as his lips grazed the next fingertip. "The wind was blowing in off the lake, molding the dress you were wearing to your thighs." A light kiss skimmed the last finger, and his teeth gently nipped at the base of her thumb. "Pink-rosebud sheets were fluttering on the clothesline behind you." He smiled as his mouth moved over her wrist. "They were the same sheets that were on your bed the first night we made love."

She whispered, "You remembered."

"Every detail of every minute." He pulled her

into his arms and kissed her good and proper. Neither paid any attention to the two giggling girls standing at the water's edge.

"Are you sure you're all right, Erin?"

She glanced up from scraping the empty pink plastic bowl with her spoon, surprised at the concern in Bain's voice. "I'm fine. Why do you keep asking?"

He looked at Arlene and Caitlin. By their innocent expression he could tell he wasn't going to get any help from that department. "First we go to dinner and you eat a total of three french fries and only sip at your drink."

"You were counting?"

He ignored her question. "Then we go to the movies and you cry when the puppies are kidnapped."

"That was sad! All those baby puppies being taken away from their mommy and daddy." She licked the plastic spoon clean and eyed Caitlin's half-eaten banana split.

"Then you cried when they were rescued."

"I wasn't crying then." She reached over and exchanged her empty banana-split bowl with Caitlin's half full one. Caitlin had finished all she could, and the remaining ice cream was beginning to melt. "Those were tears of joy, so that doesn't count as crying." She dug into the vanilla ice cream covered with pineapple syrup.

Bain frowned. "When I asked what was wrong at dinner, you said something about coming down with a bug."

The white plastic spoon sliced into the banana. "So?"

"Then at the movies you ate a large popcorn, three boxes of Milk Duds, and drank a soda."

A frown creased Erin's brow as she dug into the remaining scoop of chocolate ice cream. "I guess I was mistaken about the bug and was hungry from missing dinner." The spoon scraped the bottom of the bowl, capturing every last drop of syrup. "Is there a point to all this, Bain?"

"I never knew you loved ice cream."

She pushed away the empty bowl. "I don't. I only eat it occasionally."

He looked at the girls for some support. None was forthcoming. "I don't mean to sound critical, Erin, but do you realize you ate your entire banana split?"

Her chin rose defiantly. "Wasn't that what you bought it for?"

"Well, yes." He shifted in his seat. "But you also finished half of Caitlin's and a good two thirds of Arlene's."

Erin stared down at the picnic table in horror.

Three empty bowls sat directly in front of her. Someone would have to run them through a dishwasher to get them any cleaner. "I did?"

"You don't remember?"

"Of course I remember," she snapped. She looked around the eating area at the other families gathered there. No one else had three empty banana-split bowls in front of them. A blush of embarrassment swept up her cheeks. "I guess I was hungrier than I thought." She took a napkin and wiped at some ice cream smeared across Arlene's cheek.

Bain chuckled, and started to gather up the trash.

"What's so funny?" Erin asked as she and the girls walked over to the car.

"I was just thinking about all those calories." He wiggled his eyebrows and hustled the girls into the backseat of his car. As he opened the passenger door for Erin, he whispered, "I was also thinking about how we could work them off."

She glanced around to make sure they weren't being overheard. "How?"

"I have never seen anyone eat strawberry sauce the way you do." He reached out and stroked her lower lip. "You close your eyes and seem to savor every drop. Even your little pink tongue sweeps across your lips to make sure you didn't miss a drop."

"Strawberry sauce, huh?" Her gaze slid hungrily down the entire length of him as she climbed into the car. Desire darkened her eyes as her gaze followed him around the car and as he got in behind the wheel.

She chuckled sinfully as the keys slipped out of his fingers when she asked, "Can we stop at a store on the way home?"

Bain reached across the bed and came up with a pillow, but no Erin. He rolled over and squinted at the illuminated red numbers on the clock. It was after three o'clock in the morning. Where was Erin? Had one of the girls woken up and he hadn't heard them? He got out of bed and slipped on his jeans. As quietly as he could, he opened the bedroom door and tiptoed down the hall. The girls didn't know he spent the nights there, and he'd really rather not enlighten them.

Both girls' bedrooms looked dark and peaceful. He was heading for the stairs when a sound from the bathroom caught his attention. He knew that sound. Erin's bug was rearing its ugly head and, by the sound of things, with a vengeance.

He waited a few minutes, then lightly tapped on the door and whispered her name.

She moaned. "Go away."

"Come on, honey, open the door."

"No, go away."

He sighed in exasperation. She sounded pitifully sick. "Come on, sweetheart. Maybe I can get you something."

She moaned again. "You can get out of here and leave me to die in peace."

He chuckled softly and leaned against the wall to wait. She couldn't be that sick if she was still sassy and spirited. "I'll help you back to bed when you're ready. Just take your time."

Bain heard the van pull into the driveway and quietly slipped from the house. Caitlin and Arlene were so busy watching cartoons that a UFO could land in the side yard and they wouldn't budge. He hurried around the porch and smiled as Erin climbed out of the van. "What did the doctor . . ."

His voice trailed off as Erin leaned against the van as if for support. He hurried forward as what little color Erin had in her cheeks drained away. "Erin, what the hell's wrong?"

Erin blinked him into focus. The keys fell from her numb fingers to land on the gravel driveway. Somewhere in the van was her purse, or had she left that in the doctor's examining room? Who knew? Who cared?

"Erin!" Bain reached out and lightly cupped her shoulders. "Erin, love, you're scaring me."

She swallowed and tried to work up some moisture for the Sahara called her throat. Her knees were shaking, chills were running up and down her spine, and her palms were coated in sweat. All in all, she thought she was handling this very well. She eyed Bain and noticed his complexion wasn't as robust as it had been a minute ago. She wanted to laugh, knowing it was going to get worse, a lot worse, but couldn't. Tears clogged her throat and flooded her eyes as she tried to whisper the words that had pounded through her mind the entire seven-mile trip home from the doctor's office. She understood the words and all their implications. Bain had lied to her. The man she loved had lied.

"Erin, say something," Bain pleaded.

She fought against the black dots swarming before her eyes. She wanted to see the look on his face when she told him. Her voice was weak and held a faraway quality to her own ears. "I'm pregnant."

She concentrated on his features. Shock and disbelief caused his face to turn a peculiar shade of white. The last thought that filtered into her mind before she passed out was, Was that a glimpse of joy she'd seen on his face?

SEVEN

Erin moaned and slowly opened her eyes. The faded, cracked ceiling of her living room came into view as the noise from the television assaulted her ears. Home sweet home.

"Erin, honey, are you all right?"

"Is she awake now?" Caitlin asked.

"Why's Mommy nighty-night?" Arlene asked.

Erin turned her head slightly and blinked at the three concerned faces surrounding her. Arlene had her thumb jammed into her mouth, a clear sign she was upset, and Caitlin's eyes were full of tears. With great effort she tried to ignore Bain, who was fanning her with a magazine and anxiously patting her hand. She pulled her hand out of his grasp and started to sit up.

"My, my, that was a nice nap." She fought a wave of nausea and smiled reassuringly at her daughters. "Did you guys behave yourselves for Bain while I was gone?"

Bain closed his eyes in disbelief as Arlene climbed up onto Erin's lap and started to tell her about a cartoon she had seen earlier. Had the whole world gone crazy, or was it just him? Erin was pregnant with his child! He wanted to dance and sing and kiss her senseless. He paced over to the window and back again. Erin looked like hell. She looked like she was about to kiss the ground again, throw up, or cry. Maybe she was going to do all three. Compared with her, Casper the Ghost looked like he'd spent a month in Hawaii.

Despite his concern, happiness bubbled forth. He was going to be a daddy! A real daddy! Wait a minute. He frowned, remembering that the doctors had told him he couldn't. But Erin was telling him he was. He wanted answers from somebody. He deserved some answers. Any kind of answers. Exasperated at being ignored, he raised his voice and shouted above the laughter bellowing from the television, "Erin!"

All three females turned and stared at him. The girls' mouths dropped open at his uncharacteristic display of impatience, and Erin just glared. "What?"

He jammed his hands into the pockets of his shorts as he studied her determined expression. Whatever was going through her mind didn't look good from his viewpoint. Where was the happiness and wonder? Erin loved children, and there wasn't a better mother this side of the Mississippi. Why wasn't she smiling, knitting baby booties, or reading a baby-names book? They had created life out of their love. He glanced at the girls as understanding dawned. They weren't married. Well, hell, that problem could be rectified with two simple words. He flashed a smile and forced himself not to jump up and down. "We need to talk." He'd be damned if he was going to propose in front of an audience.

Erin's eyes narrowed and her chin rose. "We'll *talk* later." Her arms tightened around Arlene. "Right now it's lunchtime."

She released Arlene and was about to stand, but Bain stopped her. "You stay put just in case you need to take another nap." He glanced meaningfully at the girls. He still didn't like the lack of color in Erin's cheeks. "I can fix lunch." He smiled brightly at the girls. "I'll have you know I can make the best peanut-butter-and-jelly sandwiches in all of New York."

He ushered the girls toward the kitchen and glanced back over his shoulder. "Put your feet up and rest. I'll bring your lunch to you."

Erin closed her eyes and curled up on the couch as everyone filed out of the room. A few minutes later her eyes popped open as Bain dashed back into the room wielding a knife and dripping grape jelly all over the place. He stared down at her in horror and sputtered, "You can't be!"

"Can't be what?"

His voice lowered to a whisper. "Pregnant."

"I assure you I am."

"But the doctors said you shouldn't."

"That's right, Bain, *shouldn't*, not couldn't."

His face flooded with guilt. They both knew he was the one who'd said "couldn't." "But . . ."

"Bain, we'll talk about this later."

"When?"

Erin closed her eyes and leaned her head against the back of the couch. With trembling fingers she started to massage her pounding temples. "Tonight after the girls go to sleep."

Bain lowered the jelly-smeared knife in frustration. She looked so vulnerable and small curled up on the end of the sofa, he hadn't the heart to push her any harder. His Erin was a fighter, a survivor, but right now she looked like a gentle breeze would knock her over. This had to have been as much of a shock to her as it had been for him. Maybe a couple hours of breathing time was what they both needed. He pushed back a strand of hair from her cheek. "Okay, honey, you win. Tonight it is." He brushed a kiss across her creased brow. "Just one more thing before I leave you in peace to rest."

"What's that?"

He stared down into huge, trouble-filled eyes. Those eyes that always seemed to be sparkling and laughing were now cloudy with distress, sadness, and uncertainty. He couldn't have picked a worse time to declare his intentions, but timing had never been his strong suit. "I love you."

Erin watched as he walked back into the kitchen. A lone tear escaped the pools gathering in her eyes. With a hard swipe she removed the sign of weakness from her cheek. "Damn." She placed her hand on her still-flat abdomen. "Double damn."

"How are you feeling?"

Erin glared at Bain and went back to tracing the wet circle her glass of ice water had left on the kitchen table. He already knew the answer to his question. He hadn't left her side all day. He had been standing outside the bathroom door that morning when she'd opened it after losing her breakfast. He was the one who'd caught her when she almost kissed the driveway after coming home from the doctor's, and he had been standing back outside the bathroom door after lunch. And wasn't he the one who'd scowled at her the entire time he scraped her full dinner plate into the garbage?

"Come on, Erin, you haven't said more than three words to me all day."

She glanced around the cleaned kitchen and sighed. It was time. The girls were in bed and safely out of earshot. She looked at Bain and hardened her heart. "You lied to me."

"Lied?"

She would have stood up and paced around the room, but her legs still felt like rubber. She hadn't been able to hold down more than a couple of crackers and some soda all day. "You didn't have to lie, Bain. I still would have gone to bed with you. We just would have used something."

"I didn't say that to get you in bed with me. In case you forgot, we had already done it twice before birth control was brought up."

She plucked a napkin from the holder sitting in the middle of the table and started to shred it into tiny pieces. "You're right." The pile of minced paper grew in front of her. "It doesn't matter, because it doesn't change the fact."

"That you're carrying my baby."

She was momentarily thrown off balance by the pain deepening his voice. "No, I was talking about the fact that you lied to me."

"I didn't lie to you, Erin. I told you what the doctors told me."

"You told me you couldn't father a child. Would

you like to call Dr. Warner? I'm sure he could enlighten you on a few facts of life." She noticed Bain's complexion darkening with anger and egged him on further. "But if you didn't lie, that only leaves one other possibility."

"What?"

"You're not the father."

Bain's face turned a molten red as he jumped to his feet. "How could you *say* that?"

"How could you *think* that?" There, the cards were out on the table, and one of Erin's worst fears was lying faceup. If Bain really thought he was sterile, he would never believe the child was his. "If you tell me you can't father a child, and I tell you I'm pregnant, that could only mean one thing: You're not the father."

He was totally speechless. His mouth fell open, but no words came out. He marched over to the sink and back again. Stopping in front of her, he scowled his displeasure. His finger shook as he pointed to her stomach. "That baby is mine and don't you ever again say it isn't!"

Erin breathed a sigh of relief. He wasn't going to disclaim their baby. The first signs of hope sprang forth in her heart. Maybe they would make it after all. "All right, Bain, I won't."

He nodded as if they were finally getting somewhere. "The doctors obviously either read my test wrong or they got my sample confused with some- one else's. I'll call my doctor tomorrow to find out what happened."

"You don't have to, Bain."

"Of course I do."

She shifted through the pile of shredded napkin in front of her. "I was scared you'd lied to me." She smiled faintly at the way he kept pacing around the room. "Sorry, but I have this thing against liars."

"I know, you told me." He walked over to the sink and looked out the window above it. "Want to tell me about it?"

"About what?"

"Who lied to you? Was it your husband?"

"No, Cameron never once lied to me. He was the sweetest, kindest man you ever would have met." She stared down at the pile of shredded nap- kin. "My father lied to us constantly. My mother used to make up excuses for him until my brother and I were old enough to see through him." Ripped paper fluttered through her fingers. "He used to promise us wonderful presents when we were kids. Then it was promises of how he was going to give up drinking, and finally the lies and the coverups. The day I graduated from high school, my mother threw him out of the house."

"I'm sorry, Erin."

"Don't be." She glanced up and mustered a

small smile. "I never could figure out why she waited so long."

Bain walked over to her and tilted up her chin. "There won't be any lies between us, Erin." He kissed away the two tears that had slipped down her cheeks, then he captured the moan tumbling off her lips with a heated kiss.

Everything was going to work out, she thought. There was no way Bain could kiss her like that and not mean forever. The baby she was carrying might push their relationship forward faster than expected, but the end results would be the same. Forever.

He abruptly released her and resumed his pacing, stalking back over to the window and staring out into the darkness. "We seemed to have gotten off the subject."

She smiled again as she stood up and leaned against the table. Bain was acting awfully nervous and jittery. "You were the one who kissed me."

He cleared his throat. "Point noted." He fidgeted with the lace trim on the curtain. "I've been thinking about this all day." The delicate lace started to wrinkle in his grip. "In fact it's all I've been thinking about since you came home from the doctor's."

Erin anxiously shifted her weight. She could smell the marriage proposal coming a mile away, and she wanted Bain to hurry up. She wanted to remember every word he uttered. Most importantly she wanted to run across the room, throw herself into his arms, and shout YES, YES, YES! She knew their marriage would need lots of patience and understanding, especially for the next nine months. Attila the Hun with PMS would seem like a lamb compared with her when she was pregnant. And then there were Caitlin and Arlene to consider. But she knew it would all work out, because she loved Bain.

"Believe me," he went on, "this is not a decision I made lightly. I weighed all the health risks involved, and I decided I couldn't live with myself if something should happen to you."

"What are you talking about?" This had to be the weirdest proposal in history.

"The baby." The delicate lace being strangled in his fist started to rip.

"What about the baby?"

"I think"—his gaze fixed somewhere over her shoulder—"you should abor . . ." He swallowed hard. "Abor . . ." He tried again. "Abor . . ." He couldn't say the word. The curtain was yanked from the window, rod and all.

Erin's hands protectively covered her abdomen. "You want me to . . . to . . . to get rid of our baby?" she asked in horror.

"Want!" he shouted. "Hell, no, I don't *want*

you to get r . . . r . . . you-know-what the baby." He dropped the curtain and took a step closer to her. "I'm trying to be sensible. What if something should happen to you? What about Caitlin and Arlene?"

"Sensible!" She backed away as he took another step nearer. "Get out of my house!" This was not the man she loved. The man she knew and loved would never even suggest such a thing. "Pack your stuff and get out of my apartment!" The kitchen was starting to spin. She blindly reached behind her for some kind of support and found nothing. "Better yet, just get out of my life!"

Bain's pale and distraught face disappeared in a swirl of bright lights and black corridors. She never heard him frantically call her name or felt his arms catch her for the second time that day.

Erin slowly opened her eyes and squinted at the flapping magazine six inches from her nose. Her eyes slammed shut as a mail-in advertisement dropped out of the magazine and bounced off her cheek. She cautiously turned her head and frowned. Bain was sitting next to her on the couch. He wasn't paying any attention to the waving magazine or to her. He was too busy going through the contents of her purse, which had been dumped all over the coffee table. Great, she thought. Wasn't it bad enough he had stolen her heart? Now he wanted her money. "The money is in the wallet. "

He jerked his head around and glared. "What's the name of your doctor?" He sifted through some scraps of paper and cursed as a half-eaten lollipop came unwrapped and stuck to his finger. "Is it Gardner? Turner?" He turned over another business card and frowned.

"Why?"

He shot her a look that clearly indicated what he thought of her intelligence—she had none. "That's the second time today you decided to take a *nap* while standing up." He opened up her wallet. A pitifully small amount of cash, a library card, a Social Security card, and over a dozen different pictures of the girls joined the pile on the table.

"You don't have to call the doctor, Bain. What's happening to me is perfectly normal."

"Normal? No way José. I have a sister and three sisters-in-law who have more babies than the old woman who lived in the shoe, and none of them ever passed out while carrying."

"I said for *me* this is normal." She started to sit up, felt the room begin to spin, and quickly laid back down.

Bain looked appalled. "You mean you do this the whole nine months?"

"Of course not. Only the first three." She fought a smile at his look of relief. "And the last three."

He gave up looking for the doctor's business card. "What else should I know about?"

"Nothing, Bain. You aren't going to be anywhere around here." She stared up at the ceiling and frowned. She'd never noticed the tiny cracks and the yellowish tint before. It looked like it could use some work.

"The hell I'm not!"

She kept her gaze glued to the ceiling. "If you would hand me my checkbook, I'll refund your security deposit."

"You really expect me to leave?" He stood up and walked to the other side of the room.

"After that comment in the kitchen, I expected you to be halfway across the state by now." She eyed a particularly long crack. It looked like the plaster would need to be touched up before she could re-paint.

Bain slowly sank into a rocking chair and eyed the woman reclining on the couch. The burden of pain, fatigue, and worry slumped his shoulders, and disappointment bowed his head. "You don't know me at all, do you?"

"No, I guess I don't."

He heard the tears clogging her throat and saw the way her hand lay over her abdomen, protecting their child. "Would you like to hear what I know about you?"

A muttered no barely reached his ears.

"I know that you will have that baby come hell or high water. I wouldn't delude myself by thinking it's just because it's mine. I know you are a wonderful mother to Caitlin and Arlene. You're incredibly sexy and smart with an amazing gift for growing things. I guess it's all bound together with the nurturing aspect you have with children." He started to rock back and forth. "I also know I'm not going any-where. I'm staying right here and taking care of you, the girls, and Junior there." He frowned as a lone tear slid down her cheek.

"I know you're scared, Erin, but not half as much as I am." He stood up and walked over to her. "I'm scared to death something is going to happen to you." He sat down on the couch and laid his hand over hers. "I'm terrified something might happen to the baby." He reached up and tenderly cupped her cheek. "Do you want to know what really frightens me?"

"What?" Erin couldn't imagine anything fright-ening Bain. He always seemed so strong and self-assured.

"That you won't love me as much as I love you."

The tears that had been building overflowed and poured down her cheeks. He had talked of love, her, the girls, and even their unborn child, but he had never mentioned marriage. How could she trust a man who one day said he couldn't father children yet three weeks later she ended up pregnant? One minute he mentioned getting rid of their baby and the next he vowed to protect it. What about his declaration of love? Where was the proposal? The bent-knee speech? The promise of forever? She wanted the forever. She wanted to be a family.

Bain gathered her up onto his lap. "It's okay, love. Everything is going to work out just fine, you'll see."

Comfort surrounded her. She needed a shoulder to cry on, and even if Bain was the cause of all her tears, it still felt wonderful to be held by him. Great, she thought, not only were her hormones bouncing off the walls, she was going nuts to boot. She wondered how she was going to hold their baby, let alone breast-feed, while wearing a straitjacket. The tears came harder as she wailed her misery into the front of his shirt.

"Come on, love, please stop crying."

"I can't." She wiped her tearing eyes with his T-shirt and hiccuped.

Bain glanced frantically around the room and held her tighter. She was ripping his heart out with each and every tear. He could understand her being upset or even mad, but the endless weeping was ripping him apart. Was she this troubled about the baby? Or was it the fact that he'd unknowingly lied about being sterile? "Come on, Erin, please talk to me."

"I can't do it," she sobbed against his chest.

"Do what?"

"Paint the ceiling!"

He studied the top of her head nestled under his chin, then glanced up at the ceiling. "You want to paint the ceiling?" he asked in confusion.

"It's yucky." She cried harder.

He rocked her back and forth and gently rubbed her back. His brothers always said that there was only one person who could understand a pregnant woman, and that was another pregnant woman. He was beginning to grasp the logic in that statement. "Why can't you paint the ceiling?"

"Fumes." The tears started to slow down. "The fumes could harm the baby."

He had no idea what the ceiling had to do with the baby, but he was encouraged that she seemed to be calming down. "How about if I paint the ceiling for you?" Hell, he'd paint every room in the house if it would make her stop crying.

"You'd do that for me?"

He cupped her chin and lifted her face out of his shirt. His fingers were tender as they wiped at the remaining tears. "Oh, love, I'd do that and a lot more. All you have to do is ask."

Everything but marry me. Erin opened her mouth to say something, but quickly closed it again. She studied his determined expression and sighed. "Thank you." She moved off his lap and stood up. "I think we should call it a night."

He released her with obvious reluctance. "You go take a nice hot shower and get a good night's sleep. I'll be bunking down here on the couch in case you need me."

"That's not necessary."

"I'll do it anyway."

She didn't have the strength to argue anymore tonight. If he wanted to sleep on a too-short, lumpy couch, that was his problem. She had enough of her own. She walked over to the stairs and gripped the banister. "Bain?"

"Yes?" he said hopefully.

"I'll understand if you aren't here in the morning."

"I'll be here," he growled.

"Ah, but for how long?" She didn't wait for his answer. Her footsteps were slow and ponderous as she trudged up the stairs.

Bain watched her go with a heavy heart. He reached out and touched the banister where her hand had been a moment before and whispered the answer he had longed to shout. "Forever, Erin, forever."

He walked over to the couch and sat back down. Why did life have to be so complicated? He listened to the bathroom door upstairs close and heard the shower start. The woman he loved was getting naked to stand under a downpour of hot, steamy water, and he was destined to spend a sleepless, lonely night on the sofa. In agony he visualized every curve that lucky bar of soap was visiting. The gentle slopes of her hips. The lush fullness of her breasts. The faint curve of her abdomen, where his baby was growing. What he thought he could never have was flourishing under Erin's heart. Their baby. Their miracle.

He tilted his head back and stared up at the ceiling as the water was shut off. Erin was right, the ceiling could use a fresh coat of paint. Was he being selfish to feel so happy? What price was Erin going to pay for his happiness? If her doctor had advised her not to have any more children, it must be serious, but how serious? If it was life-threatening, he would have to risk her anger again and bring up the subject she didn't want to hear about. Hell, he didn't want to hear it either. It had ripped his heart to shreds even thinking about it. He hadn't even been able to say the words. But he had to make Erin understand she was more important than his dream of holding a wailing newborn in his arms. They already had two beautifully healthy daughters, and he would never forgive himself if something happened to Erin.

The bathroom door opened, footsteps padded across the hall, then the bedroom door closed. Bain scowled as he glanced around the living room. He didn't want to be there. He wanted to be upstairs snuggled under the light blankets, declaring his love, and begging Erin to prove that dreams really could come true.

What would happen if he went upstairs and asked Erin to marry him? Would she agree just because she was pregnant? Wasn't that the reason he had been holding off any declarations of further commitments? He wanted Erin to love him for himself and not because he was Caitlin and Arlene's father. Now, with the added presence of Junior, the situation had gone from complicated to mass confusion.

How was he ever going to straighten out his own feelings toward Erin? He'd been having difficulties before separating Erin the woman from Erin the mother. Now it was a total impossibility. Erin was carrying his dream deep within her womb.

What he needed was more time. They needed more time. She obviously didn't really know him at all if she actually thought he would leave. He needed to prove to her that he wasn't going anyplace. He was going to be staying right there, loving and protecting her and their unborn child and taking care of the girls. Time was his worst enemy and his best friend. The secret to a happily-ever-after ending was not to rush into anything. Erin was his main concern. She had a lot more to deal with now. He had to give her the extra time, be patient, and not push her into making any major decisions.

He muttered a curse as he got off the couch and locked up for the night. Eventually he found a small pillow in the shape of a duck and a pink blanket stowed away in a toy box in the corner of the room. With a few more muffled curses directed at the too-short couch, miniature blankets, and fuzzy ducks, he lay down on the couch for a long, sleepless night.

EIGHT

Erin sat on the edge of the tub and pressed a cold washrag to her face. So much for the toast and tea she had had for breakfast. Obviously Junior had the same discriminating taste buds as his sisters. Whatever went down must come up. It was the law of gravity in reverse.

She placed a reassuring hand over her stomach and mustered a smile. Somehow it had sounded right when Bain had referred to their child as Junior. Maybe it was a boy. He'd have his father's deep-green eyes, red hair, and wicked smile. Erin laughed softly as she stood up to face the mirror hanging on the back of the door. She had just described Caitlin. Boy or girl, chances were it would have those features. They all had the same father and mother.

She pulled the cotton nightgown taut against her body and critically studied her reflection. Five weeks pregnant didn't inspire great changes in her body yet. It still looked the same. Maybe her breasts were a tiny bit larger, but that could be wishful thinking on her part. The scale had pointed to a loss of two pounds in the past week, but she couldn't detect it. Experience had taught her to expect some weight loss in the beginning before the enormous gain. By the ninth month she would have to be standing three giant steps away from the mirror to see her entire bulk. Mother Nature had a sick sense of humor.

She released the nightgown and reached for her toothbrush. She knew Bain was standing outside the bathroom door, having appeared there moments after she had run into the room and locked the door. A person deserved some privacy, and she was thankful he had realized that and had refrained from pounding on the door demanding to know if she was all right. In a way it was sweet of him to be so caring, following her to the bathroom every time she was sick. She should think about putting a chair in the hallway for him. He at least deserved to be comfortable. Maybe she should place a pile of magazines there too.

A sleepless night of tossing and turning had brought her no closer to understanding their relationship. The past two years had been a slow, gentle rocking of life, a time for healing and reflecting. A time for loving her daughters and thinking about their future. She'd survived on a day-to-day basis, with hardly a wave to topple her peaceful existence. While she should have been battening down the hatches and guarding her heart, a typhoon had swept in and capsized her life. In less than two months she had met Bain, taken him on as a tenant, fallen in love, and become pregnant. With hurricane-force winds he had swept into her life and thrown her off course. She felt like she was in the middle of the ocean floundering. She had no idea which direction the current would take her next.

She loved Bain, and he said he loved her. They had created life together, and he appeared to make a wonderful father for her daughters. So where was the storybook ending? Where were the I dos and the happily-ever-after? Was he scared of the commitment? If that were the case, why hadn't he run like hell yesterday when she'd announced she was pregnant, instead of pacing a hole in the rug outside the bathroom door?

Her face and teeth were clean, her hair was neatly braided, and short of slapping herself silly, she had all the color in her cheeks she was going to get. Her stomach had settled down to just plain queasy. After a final look in the mirror she sighed, opened the door, and faced a worried-looking Bain. She lifted one eyebrow, as if in surprise. "Good morning, Bain. Did you sleep well?"

"By the look of things," he said, brushing a finger across the deepening circles under her eyes, "I'd say better than you."

"Full of compliments this morning, aren't we." She walked over to her bedroom door. "Was there any particular reason you were sleeping on the living-room floor?"

"Your couch is too short." He leaned against the doorjamb and blocked her way into the room. "I guess I should be thanking you for covering me up with that quilt this morning."

She'd practically had to step over him to get into the kitchen earlier, and he had looked awfully cute trying to fit his entire six-foot-long body under one of Arlene's baby blankets. "Is there something wrong with the bed in your apartment?"

"Yeah." A devilish grin spread across his face. "You weren't in it."

"I wasn't on the living-room floor either." She nervously toyed with the sash on her robe. She didn't like that grin. That was the same grin that had gotten her into this awkward situation.

"Is that an invitation?" he asked.

"No." She tried to squeeze by him and ended up brushing her body against the length of his. Heat and desire overruled the queasiness in her stomach, and every one of her hormones started to sizzle. Her treacherous body remembered the loneliness of her bed last night.

Bain tenderly cupped her shoulder and stopped her retreat. The desire darkening his gaze reflected her own. "Erin?"

"Yes?" she asked hopefully.

He pressed his hand against her abdomen. "I missed you last night."

"You did?"

His hand stroked the curve of her hip. "Your couch is lumpy and your floor is hard."

She dropped her gaze in disappointment and backed away from his caress. Was that all it was between them, sex? "You could have gone to your apartment to sleep. No one told you to sleep on the floor."

Bain sighed in defeat and leaned against the jamb. He wanted to pick her up, lay her across her bed, and make slow, sweet love to her. "What if you needed me? What if you decided to take another nap standing up?"

"I was in bed sleeping, Bain. I hardly think I would be waking up to pass out."

He jammed his hands through his hair in frustration. She was too stubborn and mule-headed for her own good. "I can sympathize with the morning sickness, but I'm a little concerned about the other hourly visits to your favorite room in the house."

"They're not hourly and they'll soon be slowing down."

"When?"

"In a couple of weeks."

"Can't your doctor give you anything?"

"I have an appointment Monday with an obstetrician, but even if he prescribes something, I won't take it."

"Why the hell not?"

"Because I don't believe in loading my body with chemicals, particularly while I'm carrying."

Bain couldn't argue that point. He himself had stopped taking all those pain pills the nurses had kept shoving at him as soon as he was able. "Okay, Erin, we'll start watching your diet."

"We?"

"Yes, *we*." He didn't like the way her chin notched upward nor the glint that appeared in her eyes, but he was fighting for his future. He had to show her he cared. "What really has me concerned is your tendency to imitate a throw rug a couple of times a day. What causes that?"

"Two things. The first is me getting up too fast or any sudden movements."

"And the second?" He didn't remember her moving fast or rising when she'd passed out before.

"Stress."

"Stress?"

"Yes, stress." Erin glanced at the clock in her room and sighed. The girls would be getting up soon and she felt like she hadn't even gone to bed yet. "When I get extremely upset about something, my body throws everything into high gear, and I kind of short out for a couple of seconds."

"You mean that if I force some major decisions on you, you'll probably try to play speed bump again?"

Her eyes narrowed. He looked guilty as sin about something. "I already told you I'm keeping the baby."

"I heard you loud and clear the first time. This is all new to me, Erin, and I'm trying to figure out the rules."

"Rules?"

"Yeah, rules. Like, are you going to require the use of the bathroom after every meal? Do you crave pickles and ice cream, and do you cry during the commercials about long-distance telephone calls? Or are you going to be totally different and walk around with a stereo system strapped across your belly so the baby can listen to classical music and foreign-language tapes?"

Erin burst out laughing at the image of her repotting geraniums with a boom box strapped to her waist.

He smiled, too, and reached out to pull her into his embrace.

She nestled against him. He felt as warm and comfortable as her empty bed across the room would. "Bain?" She promised herself one more minute of heaven before she pushed him away. Her heart was telling her it wasn't all sex and guilt on his part. Could he possibly love her as much as she loved him? Could the fairy-tale ending still be within her grasp?

"Hmmm?"

"The girls will be getting up any minute." She pushed herself out of his arms.

He tilted up her chin and studied her face. "You still look like hell."

"Really, Bain, you have to stop all this flattery. It's going to my head."

He placed a light kiss on her mouth. "How about if I make the girls breakfast and take them over to the apartment for a couple of hours while you crawl back into bed and catch up on some sleep?"

Temptation was a downy-soft pillow and peace and quiet. This would be the perfect opportunity for Bain to see what the next eight and half months were going to be like. If he could stick it out for even a couple of weeks, it had to be true love. "What about your writing?"

"I'm sure I can find something to occupy them while I write."

"You're planning to write while they're there?" she asked in astonishment. Bain obviously hadn't been exposed to Caitlin and Arlene as much as she thought.

"Sure, why not?"

She forced herself to keep a straight face. "No reason." She figured a half an hour of sleep was better than none. Bain would be banging on her bedroom door within thirty minutes of putting his first piece of paper into his typewriter. She gently pushed him out of the bedroom and into the hallway. "Thanks a lot, Bain. Make sure you call me if you need any help."

Bain blinked twice as the bedroom door closed. He had expected an argument from Erin. A grin broke across his face as the door reopened and Erin stuck her head out. Here it came, he thought.

"Oh, by the way," she said, "make sure Arlene doesn't feed the kitten any cereal."

"Why?"

"It makes her gag."

"Arlene?"

"No, silly, the kitten." The door closed again, leaving him with the sinking feeling he might have bitten off more than he could chew.

Erin was chuckling as she climbed the stairs to Bain's apartment. The loud blaring of cartoons was drowned out by the boisterous argument her girls were having. Exactly what they were arguing about wasn't apparent, because the only words she could hear were "It's mine. Is not. Is too." How in the world could Bain stand all the noise? Was he deaf? A horrible thought struck her as she dashed up the rest of the steps. What if something had happened to him?

Her knock went unanswered, so she hurriedly opened the door and nearly had a coronary. Bain's apartment looked like it had just sustained a visit from *Cat in the Hat* along with *Thing One and Thing Two*. Coloring books and crayons were scattered around the room. Play-Doh was globbed and smeared across the dinette set. Dirty dishes, empty potato chip bags, and half-eaten cookies littered every surface in the room. Caitlin and Arlene were bouncing on the couch fighting over the remote control and the Coyote and Road Runner were duking it out at full volume.

In the midst of all the confusion sat Bain. He was wearing huge black earphones and facing the sliding glass doors with his back toward the room. With two fingers he was steadily pecking out words on a battered typewriter. Piles of papers and books overflowed the card table he was using as a desk.

Erin closed the door behind her and made her way to the television. With a push of a button she plunged the room into an eerie silence broken only by the unrhythmic clacking of the typewriter's keys and some other mysterious swishing sound. Both girls immediately stopped their jumping and stared in shock at their mother, who seemed to have materialized in front of them. Without saying a word, Erin pointed to the couch. Both girls instantly parked their butts on the smashed cushions.

Erin turned her head toward the swishing sound and slowly made her way to the bathroom. She stepped over two towels lying on the floor and turned off the water that had been left running in the sink. The bathroom had fared no better than the rest of the apartment. One of her daughters had discovered a new purpose for shaving cream, and by the white foam that had been smeared down Caitlin's shirt she didn't have to guess which daughter.

A black cloud darkened her face as she marched back into the living room and over to the stereo. She wasn't sure who she was madder at, the girls for single-handedly trashing Bain's apartment or Bain for allowing them to do it. She studied the controls on the stereo for a full minute before giving up. She had no idea how to turn it off, so she grabbed the earphone plug and gave it a yank.

Bain jerked his head toward the stereo when the music abruptly ended. A smile lit his face. "Erin, you're up!"

She glanced at the clock hanging on the kitchen wall. Sure enough it was reading the same time as hers back in the house. It was one o'clock in the afternoon. She had slept over five hours straight and had felt wonderful for the first time in days—until she had entered this mess. "So it seems."

He frowned at the obvious displeasure in her voice. His glance shot from the swinging earphone plug in her hand to the girls angelically sitting on the couch. Understanding began to dawn as he glanced around the room. "Now, Erin, it's not as bad as it appears."

"No?"

"No." He stood up and stretched. "The girls and I have this understanding," he said as he walked over to the sofa. "Don't we, girls?"

Caitlin and Arlene glanced between their mother and Bain.

"And what would that be?" Erin asked curiously.

"The agreement was that whatever they got out and messed up they would put away." Bain pulled a partially melted chocolate chip from Arlene's hair and casually dropped it into his empty coffee cup, which was sitting next to the typewriter. "Right, girls?"

Both girls nodded in unison.

Erin removed a magazine, an empty chip bag, and a yellow crayon from a chair and sat down. She crossed her arms and smiled sweetly at her daughters. "Well, you'd better get started. It's past lunchtime."

Caitlin turned a funny shade of green at the mention of food, but started to pick up the coloring books. Arlene looked completely lost until Bain leaned down and whispered something about crayons.

Erin hid her smile as Bain filled the kitchen sink with soapy water and started to load in the dirty dishes. She had to admit they all were doing an admirable job of straightening up the place. Watching the girls struggling to clean up their own mess was the perfect solution. Maybe next time they'd think twice before acting like a bunch of wild Indians. "So, Bain, did you get a lot of writing done?"

He flushed guiltily. "About five pages." He left the washed dishes dripping in the rack and started to wipe down the counters. "I must say that sleep agrees with you."

"Thank you." She noticed that he had showered, shaved, and changed since that morning. She wondered if it had been her daughters or he who had left the towels on the bathroom floor.

"Have you eaten anything yet?"

She knew what he was asking. He wanted to know if she'd spent any more time in the bathroom. "Six crackers and a glass of soda."

"What about lunch?"

"That was lunch." She got up and started to help the girls finish putting away the Play-Doh. Half of the multicolored globs ended up in the garbage.

"You're not going to be working in the greenhouses today, are you?" Bain asked.

"Of course I am."

"Do you think you should?"

"It's my business, Bain. It's how I put food on the table and clothes on our backs." She jammed the cans of Play-Doh into a bag along with a handful of coloring books and two boxes of crayons.

"Maybe you should think about taking it easy for a while."

"I'm only going to be repotting some plants and getting some orders ready for delivery tomorrow, not lugging around forty-pound shrubs and shoveling two tons of peat." She righted a chair and used a fingernail to scrape a hunk of Play-Doh out of the crack running down the middle of the table. She didn't want to discuss her business and what she should and should not be doing. Her dream of expanding the business had to be temporarily put on hold. She had no idea how she was going to manage to keep what she already had running, let alone expand it.

"Well, that's good." Bain refolded a hand towel for the third time. "Maybe you can stick around the last greenhouse this afternoon."

She froze in the act of handing Caitlin the bag. Slowly she turned and faced Bain. "Why, pray tell, would I want to do that?"

He folded the towel into quarters this time. "Because that's where I'll be replacing some more windows."

"Are you suggesting that I'm not capable of working alone?"

"Come on, Erin, I'm not saying that at all."

"Then what exactly are you saying?"

He threw the towel onto the counter and bellowed, "I'm saying that I care about you, Erin!"

She stared at him in disbelief for a full minute before yanking open the door and shoving the girls out onto the deck. "Well, Mr. Bain O'Neil, you sure have a strange way of showing it!" The slamming of the door shook the entire boathouse down to its foundation.

Bain shook his head to relieve the ringing in his ears and opened the door. A splinter embedded itself in the bottom of his foot as he hurried out onto the deck. Erin, who was carrying Arlene and dragging Caitlin by the hand, was already halfway across the yard. He leaned over the railing and yelled, "Stress, Erin! Remember the stress!"

Her voice carried across the yard like the battle cry of a Celtic warrior. "Stuff it, O'Neil!"

Bain hobbled over to the folding chair and sat down. His head was pounding, his foot was throbbing, and he had absolutely no idea what he had done wrong.

Erin glanced down at the two mutilated peanut-butter-and-jelly sandwiches in front of her and grimaced. Caitlin and Arlene's lunch looked about as appealing as swamp cabbage. She carefully took a knife and started to trim off the crust, just the way they liked it. The girls didn't deserve to be dragged into her problems. Her vicious mood swings had nothing to do with them and everything to do with their newest stepsibling and Bain.

He had said he cared, but it had to be a lie. If he really cared that much about her and the baby, why didn't he do the honorable thing and ask her to marry him? She was a reasonably attractive woman. At least she'd been until the pregnancy had started to take its toll. She was fairly intelligent, owned her own business, and even knew how to cook. Her daughters could either be an asset or a hindrance depending on one's outlook. By all indications Bain's outlook should be more than favorable concerning the girls. The lovemaking between them was mind-boggling, and they even had friendly conversations when they weren't in bed together. They had more going for them already than any married couple she could name.

Had he lied when he told her he loved her too? Did he honestly think she needed to hear those words just because she was pregnant? Was there anything real between them? Maybe it was all one-sided—hers. Maybe she had imagined the sparks, the laughter, the desire. Maybe her need to be part of a real family again had surfaced unconsciously and she had latched on to the first man who came along.

She sniffled and carefully placed a small handful of potato chips on the plates next to the sandwiches. She tried to be inconspicuous as she reached for another tissue to blow her nose and dry her eyes. The girls had been meekly sitting at the kitchen table for the past five minutes, waiting for their lunch and not saying a word. If she could just manage to stop the tears enough to see, they might get it sometime before dinner.

She gingerly set a plate in front of each girl. The room was starting to sway back and forth. "How about Mommy gets you both a glass of milk and then I'm going to lie down on the couch for a little while."

"Okay," Caitlin said.

"Got ya'," Arlene said.

Erin plastered on a sick-looking smile as she pulled down two plastic cups from the cabinet and placed them on the counter. All she had to do was pour the milk and she was home-free. She didn't understand what was happening to the room. Everything was getting real strange. The floor seemed to be buckling under her feet, and black dots were dancing before her eyes. A cold sweat broke out on her whole body as she clutched the counter with both hands.

"Caitlin, honey." Her voice sounded to be coming from a great distant. She put all her energy into her last two words. "Get Bain." The miniature black dots stopped swarming and opened up into a huge black void, blocking out the kitchen. Erin knew she was going to fall into that void and couldn't stop it. Her hands slipped off the counter, and she started to fall.

She kept falling and falling and falling. . . .

NINE

"Do you have any other questions, Mrs. Flynn?"

Erin laid a trembling hand across her stomach and smiled. "No, Dr. Priceman, I think you answered them all for now."

The elderly doctor glanced up from the chart he had been reading and studied her. "Your obstetrician from New York City faxed me your records last night. I might say, Mrs. Flynn, that you're either very courageous or a masochist to want to put yourself through this again."

Erin's smile was radiant. The baby was fine. "Nothing good in life ever comes easy, Doctor."

He chuckled. "I wouldn't turn down winning the lottery."

"Neither would I." She laughed along with the doctor. Today was a perfect day to believe in miracles. The sun was shining and she *and Junior* were going home in about an hour.

A light knock sounded on the closed hospital-room door. The doctor smiled at his patient and called, "Come in."

Bain walked into the room carrying a dozen red roses and a small suitcase. His gaze went instantly to the woman sitting up and smiling in bed. His throat clogged with feelings he didn't know how to put into words. He had never in his life been more scared than when Caitlin had come running out of the house the day before, screaming his name. The alarm of finding Erin passed out on the kitchen floor had turned to pure terror when he'd noticed the traces of blood on her skirt and he'd been unable to revive her. The next two hours of his life had passed in a daze as he and the girls had followed the ambulance to the hospital and the waiting had begun. When Dr. Priceman had entered the waiting room and told him Erin was fine, he nearly kissed the man in relief. But when the doctor had added that their baby was alive and healthy, he hadn't tried to contain himself. He'd hugged the doctor to within an inch of his life.

Dr. Priceman smiled at Bain and the roses but took a protective step backward. "Ah, just the man I wanted to see."

Bain tore his gaze away from Erin. "Me?"

"I already gave instructions to Mrs. Flynn, but I want to explain them to you so you can make sure she follows them."

Bain ignored the murderous glare Erin cast his way. "You have my guarantee that she will follow them to the letter."

"Good." The doctor hid his chuckle by flipping through some papers attached to the clipboard. "The first and most important is Mrs. Flynn is to have complete bed rest for the next two weeks. She may only get up to use the facilities."

Bain absently handed the roses to Erin and placed the suitcase at the foot of the bed. He started to write down the list of instructions and dietary recommendations. Dr. Priceman handed him prescriptions for prenatal vitamins, special iron tablets, and folic acid pills. The doctor went on to explain about some tests he would be scheduling later on in the pregnancy, various warning signs to be aware of, and even an herbal tea that might calm her stomach down enough for her to eat.

By the time the doctor was gone, Bain's fingers were cramped from writing, but he was smiling. With a lot of precautions and loving care Erin and the baby should make it through the next eight and a half months without any major complications.

"Well, if you two don't have any more questions, I have other patients to see." Dr. Priceman closed Erin's chart and smiled at her. "You, young lady, I will see you in my office in two weeks."

Erin returned his smile. "Yes, sir."

The doctor glanced at Bain. "And you, young man, take good care of our patient."

"You can count on that, Doc."

"There was never any doubt, son." He opened the door, but turned around when Bain called his name.

"Dr. Priceman?"

"Yes?"

Bain locked his gaze with the doctor's. "Thanks," he said, and there was a wealth of meaning behind that one word.

The doctor nodded in understanding. "It was my pleasure, son." He walked out of the room and closed the door behind him.

Rather than looking at Bain, Erin stared down at the roses, her fingers pleating the green tissue paper surrounding them. "I guess I could call my mother and see if she'd stay with me for the next couple of weeks."

Bain leaned against the door and crossed his long legs at the ankle. "If you want your mother to stay with *us*, I have no objections."

She shuddered at the thought of having her mother fussing over her and the girls for two weeks. By the time she would be allowed out of bed, her kitchen cabinets would all be reorganized, the girls' clothes would all have name tags sewn into them, and she would have drunk enough chicken broth to flood Hoover Dam. "What I'm trying to say, Bain, is that you don't have to stay."

He drew in a deep breath as if to calm himself. "I know what you're beating around the bush about, Erin. But for the last time, I will be staying. I was there for the conception, I'll be there for the birth, and I most assuredly will be there for his or her first day of school, high school graduation, and wedding. We will be sitting together on the porch overlooking the lake in matching rocking chairs rocking our grandchildren to sleep."

Erin held her breath and waited. When he didn't add anything to that suggestive statement, she sighed and glanced away. The doctor had warned her against stress. Wishing for the impossible was one sure way to induce anxiety. "Okay, I won't call my mother yet. We'll see how it works out." She toyed with the red satin ribbon tied around the roses. "Where are the girls?"

"Outside, at the nurses' station. Arlene had everyone from the evening shift wrapped around her little finger last night, so she's working on the morning shift now."

Erin smiled. "And Caitlin?"

"She's out there with pencil and paper revising

her Christmas list. It seems your daughter wants to be a doctor when she grows up."

"Last year she wanted to be a tourist."

"A tourist?"

"She saw some commercials with people lying around on beaches having a great time and asked what they were doing. I explained they were tourists on vacation and that was what tourists did. So she decided that was exactly what she wanted to be when she grew up, a tourist."

Bain laughed. "There's nothing wrong with that kid's logic." He reached over and opened the suitcase. "I packed you something to wear home. I hope I remembered everything you said to bring."

She glanced at the suitcase. It didn't matter to her what was in it. "I'm sure you did." She shifted nervously on the bed. Bain was staring at her with such an odd expression. "What's the matter?"

"I want to kiss you."

Delight tickled her stomach. "What's wrong with that?" She had been thinking the same thing since he walked into the room.

"I'm afraid."

"Of what?"

"I'm afraid that once I hold you, I'll never let you go again." He moved closer and took the flowers out of her hands. "You scared the living hell out of me yesterday."

"Sorry, I didn't mean to."

He sat down on the edge of the bed and tenderly pulled her into his arms. "Just don't do it again."

She snuggled deeper into his embrace and allowed herself a few moments of paradise. "I'll try not to." She was fine, and Junior was healthy. The girls were outside the door stealing hearts, and the man she loved had just vowed to be around forever. What more could she want out of life? She ignored the little voice screaming in the back of her head as Bain raised her chin and kissed her.

Bain pushed a stack of books and magazines off the nightstand and carefully set down the tray containing Erin's lunch.

"I just got off the phone with Mrs. Williams," she said.

He picked up one of the carrot sticks from the tray and started to munch. So far that day he had only gotten done half of what he needed to do and absolutely nothing of what he wanted to do. It was already twelve-thirty and he barely had time to fix Erin and the girls' lunch, let alone actually eat a meal himself. "Who's she?"

"The woman who owns Fingerwood Florist."

"Ah . . . I thought the name sounded familiar. Didn't I just make a delivery there this morning?"

"Uh-huh."

He raised a brow and reached for a celery stick. "Was there a problem?"

"You could say that." Erin peeked between the two pieces of whole-wheat bread and groaned. Chicken salad again. A stack of carrot and celery sticks overflowed a small plate. An eight-ounce glass of low-fat milk and a shiny red apple completed the healthy lunch. She would have sold her soul for a hot-fudge sundae smothered in walnuts and a huge slice of chocolate cake. "It seems you delivered a half dozen tiger lilies instead of the day lilies they ordered."

"You told me the orange ones."

"I know, it was my fault. They're both orange." She leaned forward and fluffed the pillows behind her. When Caitlin and Arlene were babies, she used to fantasize about being confined to bed. Cotton sheets, downy pillows, and endless hours with nothing to do but sleep had sounded like heaven. The past few days had proved that reality never quite matches up with fantasy. She couldn't find a comfortable way to sit because her butt was sore, and she was sick to death of wearing nothing but nightgowns. She had only spent three days in bed and already she was losing her mind. She kicked the sheet and light blanket to the foot of the bed in frustration. "This isn't going to work."

Bain didn't answer right away. Seeing his gaze travel hungrily up her legs, from her bare feet to the outline of her thighs beneath her cotton gown, she hastily pulled the sheet back up. Bain was looking at her the same way she would be looking at a triple-decker banana split.

Regretfully he lifted his gaze to her face. "What's not going to work?"

"You handling the business." She set the tray on her lap, then fidgeted with the paper napkin and restacked the carrot sticks. "It's not that I don't appreciate everything you've been doing for the past three days, Bain. You're doing a wonderful job taking care of the girls and me."

"Thanks." He sat down in a chair next to the bed and scowled at the sheet.

"The house still seems to be standing, but I'm beginning to worry."

"About what?"

"You." She took a bite out of the sandwich and resigned herself to another healthy lunch.

"Me?"

She swallowed and waved the partially eaten sandwich in his direction. "No offense, Bain, but you're beginning to look like hell."

His shoulders straightened in defense. "What's this, pay-back time for last week?"

"No, I'm just calling the shots as I see them. When was the last time you wrote?"

"Last night, after you and the girls were asleep."

"You were up here last night watching the late news with me." She munched on a carrot stick. "Let me see if I have this right. First thing in the morning you feed everyone breakfast and then do my work in the greenhouses and make the deliveries. Then it's lunch and back to the greenhouses to replace some more glass and do the daily watering. For the last three days you have also been keeping up with the girls' swimming lessons, fixing dinner, cleaning house, and giving the girls baths." She punctuated the air with a half-eaten carrot stick. "Are you trying for the role of Superdad?"

"No. I'm just trying to keep everything going for the next two weeks."

"Well, by the looks of things my business will be in bankruptcy by my second trimester, your novel will probably read like a grocery list, and your mind will have turned into Silly Putty by the time Junior makes his or her appearance. He'll come into the world with his father standing in the corner of the birthing room pressing his forehead against the comics from the Sunday newspaper."

Bain chuckled at her description. "Any helpful hints from the peanut gallery would be greatly appreciated."

She smiled sadly as she finished off her sandwich. "I wish I had some." She took a sip of milk and frowned. "I don't see any way for me to run the business from this bed. Everything will just have to wait for another eleven days. I know you're trying your hardest, and I really appreciate it, Bain. But face it, you aren't horticulturally inclined."

"Are you saying I'll never have a green thumb?"

"Bain, not only are your thumbs brown, but your eight fingers are too. You can't tell the difference between a pansy and a petunia. You needed to look up a picture of a geranium in your encyclopedia before loading up a dozen for delivery." She smiled good-naturedly. "Your two good qualities are your willingness to work and the fact that you aren't color-blind."

He playfully tossed a magazine at her. "At least I have two good qualities."

She caught the magazine with one hand and steadied her glass of milk with the other. "Are you saying I don't?"

"I would never be that ungallant."

"But you're insinuating I don't."

He cocked an eyebrow and grinned, then swiped the last celery stick when she reached for the apple. "So what can we do about your precious plants?"

"I made a deal with Mrs. Williams. Her shop

will be picking up her deliveries for the next two weeks."

"At a loss to you?"

"For a reasonable discount. This way they're sure to get the correct plants." She wiped her mouth with the napkin. "The only other thing I could think of is for you to bring me the plants that look sick to you."

"In your bedroom?"

"Yes. That way I can try to keep the remaining inventory alive and healthy until I get back on my feet." She set the tray back on the nightstand. "Is there a problem?"

"Uh, no." He handed her back the nearly full glass of milk. "Drink it."

"You know I don't like milk, Bain."

"Doc said three glasses a day, love." He tried not to laugh at her look of distress. "Bottoms up."

Erin downed the entire glass without stopping and handed the empty glass back to Bain. "If I have to drink any more milk, I swear I'll grow udders."

Bain's gaze dropped immediately to the front of her gown. Delicate lace and ribbons added a touch of sensuality to the plain cotton gown. His fingers itched to undo the three tiny white buttons that held the gown closed over her breasts. He wanted to fill his hands with her sweetness and to taste their forbidden fruit once again. He glanced at his watch. It had been five days, fourteen hours, and thirty-six minutes since he had felt the incredible sweetness of Erin wrapped around him. Appalled at this own body's reaction, he quickly picked up the empty tray and straightened the pile of books he had knocked over earlier. "Don't worry, Erin. Between us I'm sure we can keep the business going for another eleven days."

"But what about your writing?"

"I'll manage something. Don't worry." He turned to the door, knowing he had better go check on the girls, who were downstairs eating their lunch. He had promised them that if they ate all their lunch and didn't bother Erin, he would allow them to eat dinner upstairs in Erin's bedroom that night.

"And your sanity?" she asked.

He chuckled. "That has to be blamed on that lumpy overgrown chair that you call a couch. You would be amazed at what a person could put up with if they had a decent night's sleep."

Erin sighed as he left. She was already lonely. She glanced around the room in dismay. Bain's color television and VCR were hooked up and sitting on top of her dresser. An easy chair from the living room had been brought up for the comfort of guests, and a radio-cassette player sat on the floor next to the bed. Magazines, books, and tapes littered every surface, and whatever they didn't manage to cover,

Caitlin's and Arlene's toys did. How could a person feel so lonely with so much?

She slowly reached out and caressed the empty side of the bed. She would have to keep her fingers crossed about the business, and she promised herself she would make it up to Bain somehow about his writing time. Her fingers stroked the sheet and she smiled. There wasn't a whole heck of a lot she could do about the first two problems, but she could resolve the third. Bain had never complained about backaches and sleepless nights while sharing her bed. They wouldn't be able to make love until after her checkup, but that didn't mean they couldn't at least sleep with each other.

Bain glanced around the kitchen in total disgust and with no idea where to begin. He and the girls had made a special dinner for Erin that night, setting up a table in her bedroom with a tablecloth and a candle. Bain was sure Erin would have preferred something chocolatey and fattening for dessert rather than the green Jell-O they'd had, but she'd gamely eaten everything.

Although Caitlin and Arlene didn't know it, the dinner had been something of a celebration. That afternoon when he had taken Erin a snack, she had invited him to share her bed at night again. She had made up some tale about his back going out and then all of her plants would surely die and go to rainforest heaven. It was as good an excuse as any, and Bain could hardly wait to rush upstairs and snuggle with her. But first the kitchen had to be dealt with.

Dirty dishes, pots, and pans were piled on every available surface. The stove was splotched with boiled-over spaghetti sauce that would take a chisel to scrape off. Arlene had gotten into something orange and had finger-painted the bottom cabinet doors, the kitten had scattered his food across the room, and Erin's once-gleaming linoleum floor was covered in muddy footprints from his frequent trips in from the greenhouses.

The sad part was that the living room looked no better. Piles of his clothes were stacked next to the toy box; blankets and pillows were scattered across the couch; and his typewriter, papers, empty coffee cups, and mounds of books had buried the coffee table. Arlene had left a towering monstrosity built out of Legos in the middle of the room and he hadn't the heart to ask her to tear it down. Caitlin's tea party for her dolls had turned into the social event of the year, and the guests had never departed.

Where was all the leisure time he'd once thought mothers had after the kids were tucked into bed? By the look of things he wouldn't feel a mattress under his poor tired body for the next ten hours. Tomorrow looked no better. The lawn needed to be cut, he still had three loads of laundry hanging on the back line from two days ago, and the kitten had an appointment at the vet's for his shots. In his opinion the physical ability of housewives was greatly underrated, and homemaking should be an Olympic sport. Scrubbing the ring out of the bathtub, washing dishes until you could see yourself in them, and removing grass stains from the backside of Arlene's shorts would make one hell of a tricathlon. Why hadn't he paid more attention in church to know if there was a saint for housewives? Right about now he could use some divine guidance.

Three hours later Bain slipped into bed next to Erin and sighed. His hands were red and dry, and his back ached from scrubbing the kitchen floor, but he had done it. The kitchen was spotless, and he was tired enough to sleep next to Erin without going out of his mind.

He reached over and gently pulled the sleeping woman into his arms. His eyes closed in anguish as she nestled closer and her bare leg slid in between his. Maybe this wasn't such a good idea. Maybe he should go start in on the living room, because his body obviously wasn't that worn out yet.

Erin snuggled deeper into his warmth and sleepily murmured his name.

He gently stroked her hair. "Shhh, go back to sleep, love."

"Thank you again for the special dinner."

"You're welcome." His fingers toyed with the red curls fanning his shoulder and chest. Lord, she felt wonderful to hold again.

"Never had SpaghettiOs by candlelight before."

He chuckled and hugged her closer. "Wait until you see what I can do with hot dogs and a can of baked beans, love."

Erin stood at the window and lifted her face toward the sun. Heat and light warmed her for the first time in eight days. Five nights of sleeping in Bain's arms had improved her health one hundred percent. She felt she could go out and conquer the world, right every wrong, save every plant in the greenhouses. Heck, the way she was feeling today, she could probably save the rain forests. She had just visited the bathroom and was on her way back to bed, when the girls' laughter from outside had drawn her to the window.

Bain was giving them another swimming lesson. Caitlin had advanced to putting her face in the water and actually trying a few strokes on her own. Arlene was still holding her nose and only dunking her head until the water touched her chin. Love overflowed her heart at the sight of her girls trying so hard to please her. Bain had told her that they were secretly practicing twice as hard so they could impress her when she was feeling better and could come down to the lake. Tears filled her eyes as she watched the girls try it one more time. They were being so good for Bain and handling her sickness well. She'd decided not to tell them about their new baby brother or sister until later, because she wasn't sure how these first few months would go. More, how was she going to explain about Mommy having a baby without being married?

Bain's boisterous laughter filled the air, and she saw him spinning Arlene around in a circle. Love surrounded the trio like a heavy cloak, leaving her feeling like some outsider looking in. She missed the fun and laughter with her daughters and the feel of rich soil between her fingers as she worked with the plants. She missed the warmth of the sun, the coolness of the lake, and the fiery heat of Bain's loving. She hated being confined and she despised this attack of self-pity.

She glanced back at the bed and groaned. It was beginning to look like a torture device worse than the rack. The only time she savored her confinement was when Bain joined her each night and held her close. The problem with that was that he seemed to be joining her later and later each night and leaving earlier and earlier. He either had to be living on pure caffeine or he had set up a cot in one of the greenhouses. By the look of the sick plants overflowing her bedroom, his sleeping in the greenhouses instead of working might not be too far off. He seemed to bring armloads of plants up to her room by the hour.

The fig standing in the corner wasn't weeping anymore, it was screaming for mercy, and the row of geraniums lining her dresser was a total mystery. She had never seen leaves turn that color before. What he had done to the iron-cross begonia could be classified as heartless, and the dozen African violets on her windowsills should be put out of their misery. If there was a Cruelty to Plant Life organization, they would surely be picketing her driveway by now. She prayed her remaining plants could hang in there for another six days.

The sheer white curtains drifted through her fingers. She pushed them aside and glanced one more time at her daughters, Bain, and the sun before climbing back into bed.

TEN

Bain took the steps two at a time, a grin spread across his face. He had solved one of their major problems—if he could convince Erin to go along with his plan. He burst into her bedroom and stopped dead in his tracks, the victorious grin sliding from his face. Erin was sitting in the middle of her bed, hugging a pillow and a box of tissues and crying her heart out.

"Erin, honey, what's wrong?" He glanced frantically around the room. Everything seemed the same as when he had last been there, about three hours earlier. "Are you in pain?"

Erin wiped her eyes and blew her nose. Her voice was watery and weak as she pointed to the television. "That's going to be me," she wailed.

Bain glanced at the set. A famous talk-show hostess was interviewing three women. "You want to have your own talk show?" With Erin's mood swings lately it was difficult, if not downright impossible, to know in which direction her thoughts were headed. Last week he had found her crying over a Rocky and Bullwinkle show, because Boris and Natasha were always so heartless to the squirrel and moose.

"No, Bain, the women." She wiped away a fresh stream of tears.

He sat on the edge of the bed and tried to concentrate on the show. He was at a total loss until they broke for a commercial and the hostess said they would be right back with her guests, "women who were dumped after they gave birth because they gained weight." Bain picked up the remote and clicked off the television. Outraged, he asked, "You really think I would dump you because you gained a few pounds carrying my child?"

Erin sniffled. "I don't just gain a few pounds, Bain. I explode into motherhood."

He smiled, pulled another tissue from the box, and handed it to her. "I wouldn't care if you got as big as the Goodyear Blimp."

"The comparison has already been made, and the blimp lost out. Everyone who knew me when I carried the girls swore the blimp was smaller." She sniffled into the tissue. "Greenpeace even wanted to have me declared as some extinct form of land whale."

Bain looked down at the floor to hide his laughter. "I think you might be overreacting just a tad, Erin. Pregnancy is a beautiful and extraordinary time in a woman's life. You're nurturing a human life in your body. A slight weight gain is expected."

"Slight? You still don't get it, do you, Bain? I'm not talking slight. By the beginning of my seventh month Omar the Tent Maker will be sewing my maternity clothes, and by the end of that month I won't be able to tie my own shoes. By the eighth month my feet won't get wet when I take a shower, and by the ninth month I won't even be able to get out of a chair without help!"

He pulled her into his arms. "Don't worry, love. I'll help you out of the chairs." He lifted her chin and wiped at the tears, then smiled suggestively. "I even volunteer to take showers with you so that I can reach all those parts the water can't."

Erin hugged her pillow tighter and leaned out of his embrace. "You don't even want me now when I'm not gigantic, how could you insinuate there would be anything more later?" Her voice broke into a heart-wrenching sob as she buried her face in the pillow.

Bain stared in shock at the woman he loved. "What in the hell are you talking about?"

She mumbled something into the depths of her pillow.

He pried the pillow away from her face and demanded, "What's this about my not wanting you?"

"You don't come to bed until hours after I'm asleep, and then you leave before the break of dawn. If you don't want to sleep with me, just say so and go sleep somewhere else."

Bain stood up and paced the confines of the crowded room. "Is that why you think I limit myself to three, four hours of sharing your bed at night?"

"What other reason could there be?" She wouldn't look at him as her finger traced one of the delicate violets printed on the pillowcase.

He ran his fingers through his hair in frustration. Lord save him from the ricocheting hormones of a pregnant woman. One minute Erin was up here laughing and throwing tea parties with the girls, the next she was crying her eyes out over some figment of her imagination. "Didn't it ever occur to you that the reason I wasn't spending a whole lot of time snuggled in your bed with you is because I want you too much?"

She hugged the pillow closer and looked up at him. "I don't understand."

"Well, that makes two of us." He returned to the bed and sat back down. "Lock those bouncing hormones away for one minute and listen. The reason I spend so little time in your bed is because you are driving me crazy. I can't sleep for wanting you. I torture myself for hours as you snuggle up against me and sleep."

"So why do you come?"

"Because the hours of sleeplessness and torture are worth it just to hold you in my arms."

She sniffled once more and threw her arms around his neck. "That's the nicest thing you ever said to me."

Bain groaned as her lips brushed against his neck. It had been too long since he'd kissed her, really kissed her. He pulled back and cupped her jaw. "I think what you need is a daily dose of loving to chase away these blues."

She gazed hungrily at his mouth. "Loving?"

He brushed his thumb over her trembling lower lip. "Well, semiloving, until the doctor gives his okay."

She playfully nipped at his thumb. "What's semi-loving?"

"It's where I drive you as much out of your mind as you have driven me out of mine." He placed a small string of kisses down her jaw toward her chin. "It's where we kiss each other senseless." He teased the corner of her tempting mouth. "It's where we both end up taking cold showers for six more days." He pressed her back onto the mattress and captured her lower lip between his teeth. His tongue smoothed over the light impressions his teeth made. "Lord, Erin, I almost forgot how delicious you taste." He captured her sweet mouth in a heart-stopping kiss. When he lifted his head, he whispered, "Almost, but not quite."

She moaned and greedily pulled his head back down. Heaven was the feel of her soft body beneath his. The kiss that had started out hot and spicy was turning into an eruption of need. Desire surged through him as he felt her trembling fingers sliding up his jean-clad thigh.

"Bain, Bain," Caitlin cried from downstairs. "Chris says he's done."

Bain shot off the bed and away from Erin as if he'd been burned. In another minute they would have been making love, with or without the doctor's permission. Lord, was he that depraved? He shot Erin a guilty glance and hurried toward the bedroom door. Caitlin was halfway up the stairs, and he could hear Arlene's and Chris's voices coming from the kitchen. "Caitlin, honey. I'm not finished talking to your mommy yet. Could you please tell Chris to get himself, Arlene, and you a soda from the refrigerator? I'll be right down."

Caitlin started back down the stairs in a rush. "Can we have cookies too?"

Bain chuckled. "Tell Chris there's a box of chocolate chip ones on top of the refrigerator. He can help himself, but Arlene and you can only have three each."

Caitlin glanced over her shoulder at him. "Okay."

He returned to the bedroom and saw Erin trying to straighten the bed and her nightgown. "Who's Chris?" she asked.

"The answer to one of our problems." He picked up the magazines that had scattered across the bed during their kiss.

"Which problem is that?"

"Your business."

"What about my business?"

"Hear me out, Erin. I can see your stubborn streak showing."

"Bain . . ."

"Chris will be a high school senior this year, he wants to major in horticulture in college, and he needs a part-time job. He's willing to work a couple hours after school and on weekends."

"What's that got to do with Flynn's Nursery?"

"I think you should hire him."

"Hire him! I can barely support myself and the girls. What do you propose I pay him with? Marigolds?"

"He's willing to work for minimum wage."

"Considering that's more than what I make half the time, that's awful nice of him."

Bain walked over to the window and looked outside. The sun was glistening off the lake, and a gentle breeze was blowing the clothes hanging on the back line. He really should take them down. Caitlin had complained that morning she was running out of things to wear. He glanced around the room at the plants sitting on every available surface. "You know, every time I walk into this room, I expect to see Tarzan."

"Bain, I'm waiting."

"What I'm nicely trying to tell you, without causing you any undo stress, is that there'll be more sick plants before you can get back to work. Hiring Chris seems the perfect solution. I told him that you'll be asking him a bunch of questions about the plants, so for the last half hour he's been walking through the greenhouses taking notes. I also told him if he passes your test and meets with your approval he has the job."

"Even if he could answer every question correctly, how will I pay him?"

Bain smiled slyly. "You could always double my rent."

"Don't tempt me."

"I mean it, Erin. Stop being so damn stubborn and accept my help." He saw the hesitation on her face. "Please."

She sighed and rubbed at her temples. "Send

Chris up and I'll talk to him." She scowled as Bain grinned. "But I'm not making any promises."

He placed a hard kiss on her mouth and dashed out of the room before she could change her mind.

That night Erin sat in the middle of the bed and braided her hair. Her gaze followed Bain as he straightened up the room. His hair was still damp from his shower, and he was wearing a pair of navy-blue gym shorts. He hadn't slept in the nude since returning to her bed. She missed the view.

"That was a rotten thing to do," she said.

He glanced up from the open drawer where he was putting away the laundry. Her lacy underwear was dangling from his hand. "What was?"

"Not telling me it was Chris Stockton from down the road you wanted me to hire."

"I didn't know that you knew him." He placed the undies neatly in the drawer.

"Of course I know him. Everyone knows Chris. He's the nicest kid in the entire county, and one of the poorest." She wrapped a rubber band around the end of the thick braid. "You knew I couldn't refuse him the job even if he didn't know diddily about plants."

Bain finished placing a stack of her nightgowns in another drawer. "Does he know anything about plants?"

"Probably more than me, but don't tell him. It would look bad for me if my first employee could outsmart me."

Bain chuckled and turned out the lights. "My lips are sealed."

Erin slid under the blanket and said seductively, "Now, that would be a shame."

He hurried into bed and pulled her into his arms. The heated kiss they shared relieved any doubts about his lips being sealed for her.

She snuggled closer and wove her fingers into the fine hair covering his chest. "Bain?"

"Hmmm . . ." His hands stroked over the curve of her hip.

"Starting tomorrow"—her lips brushed his collarbone—"your rent has doubled." She nuzzled his throat as his laugh filled the room.

Bain looked down at Caitlin and his half-full grocery cart and shouted, "What do you mean you don't know?" His gaze quickly shifted back down the aisle of cereals and cake mixes. Arlene was nowhere in sight.

Caitlin backed away and bumped into the metal cart. She blinked her eyes and sniffled. "She's gone."

He tossed the box of Bunchy, Crunchy, and

Munchy cereal he and Caitlin had been arguing about into the cart. Erin was never going to approve of the sugar-coated, high-fat, low-nutrition cereal Caitlin had been pleading with him to buy. She also wasn't going to be too happy if he came home without Arlene. He grabbed the cart and headed for the next aisle. Where could she have disappeared to so fast? Where would *he* go if he were almost three years old?

By the sixth aisle his initial anger had turned to fear. Ice-wrenching fear. He had lost his daughter! He nearly sprinted to the next aisle, dragging the cart and a frightened Caitlin with him. He scanned the frozen-food section. Nothing. Keeping one eye toward the registers and the doors, he dashed to the next aisle. Nothing but a mother with two screaming kids and box after box of cookies.

Caitlin was openly crying now as he headed for the last aisles. What was he going to do if she wasn't there? Could she have been kidnapped while Caitlin and he had argued over a stupid box of cereal? Some hot-shot undercover agent he was! He couldn't even go grocery shopping without losing a kid. He had failed at being a daddy.

He wheeled into the last aisle and scanned the length of it. His breath gushed out in relief as he spotted Arlene sitting in the middle of the aisle surrounded by a mountain of colorful book bags. He dashed to her, picked her up, and squeezed her tight.

Arlene grinned up at him when he finally released her and sat her back down on her feet. "Me go to school too?"

Bain glanced down at the backpacks scattered on the floor. Arlene wanted a book bag just like Caitlin's. He should have seen something like this coming by the way Arlene sulked every time Caitlin pulled out her multicolored book bag and paraded around the yard.

"No, Arlene. You can't go to school for a couple of years yet." He forced his voice to be sterner. "What you did was very bad."

Her tiny chin started to quiver. "Me no bad, Bain."

"Yes you were." He started to pile the bags back onto the shelf. "You never should have wandered away from me. Caitlin and I were very worried about you. We thought we lost you." He glanced over at Caitlin and frowned. She was still silently crying and clutching the metal cart with her little hands.

"Me no lost. Me here." Arlene handed Bain a bright-green book bag. "Me want this one."

Bain looked at Arlene and then at the bag. Gathering all his strength, he said, "No," and placed the bag on the shelf with all the rest.

Arlene's lower lip trembled, and tears filled her

eyes. She pulled the bag back off the shelf and hugged it. "Me no bad." The tears started to roll down her face. "Please."

A father would have picked up the bag and placed it in the cart, Bain thought. What was a few bucks anyway? But a daddy knew he had to stand firm and be a guiding hand in Arlene's young life. She had many lessons to learn, and most were going to cost more dearly than a book bag.

"I said no, Arlene." He took the bag from her and placed it back on the shelf. "I told you not to wander off and you did. You could have gotten lost or hurt." He picked her up and sat her in the cart. "Maybe the next time you'll be a good girl." He reached into the cart and opened the package of napkins he was going to buy. He held one to Arlene's nose. "Blow." He silently chuckled at the loud honking sound she made. So much for his daughter being delicate.

He reached for another napkin and passed it to Caitlin. He waited until she'd dried her eyes, then squatted down to her height. "It's okay, Caitlin, we found her."

Caitlin's voice quivered. "I didn't mean to lose her."

Bain hugged her. "Oh, honey, you didn't lose her, I did."

Tiny fingers clung to his shirt. "You yelled at me."

"Caitlin, I didn't mean to. I yelled at you because I was upset at Arlene for wandering off. She could have gotten seriously hurt or lost." He lifted her chin and said, "I'm sorry I yelled at you."

Caitlin blew her nose and handed him the soggy napkin.

He looked at it and smiled. Somehow he felt as if he had just passed some test. "Am I forgiven?"

Her arms encircled his neck and she kissed his jaw. "Yes." She climbed on the metal frame of the cart and pulled out the box of Bunchy, Crunchy, and Munchy. "I don't want it anymore."

Bain looked at the box and shook his head. Was there ever a greater love between two sisters? "That's very nice of you, Caitlin, but I'll buy the cereal anyway. Arlene's the one who has the lesson to learn, not you." He placed the box back in the cart. "Besides, what would you two eat tomorrow morning?"

Both girls looked at each other and smiled. Tomorrow morning was Erin's doctor's appointment, and he wanted everything perfect. The house was getting a complete overhaul that afternoon, the hamper was empty, and by the time he unloaded all this food, the cabinets would be full.

Twenty minutes later he piled all the bags into

the van and made sure the girl's seat belts were secure. He climbed into the driver's seat and started the engine.

"Bain?" Caitlin asked.

"What, honey?" He glanced behind him and started to back out of the parking space.

"Do daddies yell at their kids?"

His foot slammed on the brake, and everyone was jerked forward. He cautiously looked at Caitlin. "What do you mean?"

"I don't remember my real daddy."

Bain felt himself start to sweat. "That's okay, honey. No one expects you to remember a whole lot. It was a long time ago."

"Do you have a daddy?"

"Yes."

"Does he yell at you?"

"Sometimes, especially when I do something I'm not supposed to. But I know he's yelling because he's afraid. Just like when I yelled at you and Arlene." He smiled at the angelic picture the girls made sitting so serenely in the backseat. "He yells for the same reason I did, because I love you both."

Caitlin grinned and dropped the million-dollar bomb. "Does that make you our daddy?"

Bain closed his eyes for a second, then opened them again. He carefully studied Caitlin's face. "Would you like me to be your daddy?"

She vigorously nodded and whispered, "Yes, please."

He felt his heart burst with love as someone started to honk his horn. He was blocking the row in the parking lot. He smiled at Caitlin and started to drive away. The entire ride home he kept glancing in the rearview mirror at her. She sat there grinning back at him.

Bain slowly lowered the typed pages of his manuscript back into the box. The first two hundred and forty-two pages of his life lay there so neatly and orderly.

A few days earlier he had run into a snag in the plot and had decided to read all that he had written, hoping to find a solution to his problem. What he had found had been completely unexpected.

When he'd started rewriting the book after moving into the boathouse apartment, he had known that his protagonist, Shamus Mulligan, was much like himself. A fictionalized version of himself. And when he'd created Fiona Muldoon, he'd know that she was modeled on Erin. What he hadn't realized was that he was infusing Shamus and Fiona's story with more love than he'd ever known in his life before meeting Erin. He wasn't just writing a suspense novel, he was writing a love story. A story about the love between a man and a woman who had no children to tie them together.

For weeks he had worried about separating Erin the woman from Erin the mother. He had just about given it up as an impossibility, but all along he had been doing it. Fiona was Erin the woman. She had all the sweet, loving qualities that Erin had, but there weren't any children in the story to complicate matters. Shamus the man loved Fiona the woman, just as he loved Erin.

It didn't matter that she was the mother of his daughters or that she was carrying his unborn baby. The woman Erin had captured his heart. He would survive life without children, but he couldn't survive without Erin.

Earlier that day, when Erin had returned from her checkup with Dr. Priceman, she had been quiet and thoughtful. She seemed to be mulling over something important. He picked up the box and left his apartment, heading for Erin and the rest of his life.

ELEVEN

Erin came down the steps and smiled at Bain. He had placed two glasses of milk and a plate of fruit on the coffee table while she had been tucking the girls into bed. "It sure feels good to tuck them in for the night." She sat down next to Bain on the couch.

"You didn't overdo it today, did you?"

"No, I'm fine."

"The doctor said you were to take it easy.

"He said I could resume normal living as long as I get plenty of rest and watch my diet." Short of coming right out and saying it, it was the best way she could think of to tell him they could resume their physical relationship.

He cleared his throat and glanced away. "Yeah, normal living."

Erin munched on an apple slice. Two weeks confined to her bed had given her a lot of time to think. Probably more time than any human had the right to have, but there wasn't a whole lot she could have done about it. The more she'd thought, the clearer it had seemed. Bain and she belonged happily married living the fairy-tale dream. She loved Bain and she was positive he loved her back. He and the girls were inseparable and he would make a wonderful father to them. The baby nestled in her womb was the living proof of their love. Bain seemed excited and nervous about Junior's impending birth. She had even caught him reading her baby-names book earlier that evening.

Everything seemed so perfect for the ideal marriage. Everything except the marriage proposal. Why hadn't he asked? It seemed like the next logical step to her. For the first week and a half she'd worried about the lack of a proposal. And then it had hit her. Why did she have to wait for Bain to pop the question? Couldn't she ask him? After all, this was the nineties. The worst he could say was no. She picked up the glass of milk. "Bain?"

He glanced at the glass she was holding. "I know, you don't want to drink your milk."

She chuckled and set the glass back down. It had been an ongoing argument for the last two weeks. He wanted her to drink the milk, and she wanted thick, rich chocolate syrup mixed in with it. Bain had won every argument. "No, it's not that."

"You *do* want to drink your milk?" he asked in surprise.

"Of course not, but I will." She picked up the milk and drank the entire glass. "There, satisfied?"

His gaze skimmed down her body. "Not by a long shot."

She blushed and straightened her skirt. His thoughts had been broadcast loud and clear. They had echoed her own, but first there was one itsy-bitsy question she wanted to ask. "There's something I need to ask you, and I'm not sure how to do it." Marriage proposals were not taught in home economics or health class. She was positive, though, that the bent-knee routine didn't apply to her.

Bain lifted an eyebrow, obviously picking up on her nervousness. "I find the best way to ask a hard question is just to come right out and ask. Clean and quick." He picked up a slice of apple.

Erin straightened her skirt once more and nodded. Clean and quick sounded like good advice to her. She cleared her throat and anxiously looked at him. "Would you marry me, please?"

The apple lodged in Bain's throat, and he started to choke.

Erin clutched and unclutched her fingers in her skirt as Bain wiped his eyes and drank his own milk. He seemed to have swallowed the piece of apple that had been stuck in his throat. "Are you all right?" she asked.

"Yes." He set his glass down and jumped to his feet. "I mean no." He paced away two steps, quickly turned back to her, and shouted, "Where in the hell did that come from?"

The color drained from her face, but she held her ground. "I just thought—"

"I was supposed to ask you that!"

She crossed her arms and snapped, "I got tired of waiting." What was he waiting for? Her to become so huge that she would need to use sails to make her wedding dress? First he avoided the subject as if it had leprosy, now he complained because she was the one to pop the question. Boy, and she thought her mood swings were wacky. She watched as he anxiously paced to the stairs and back, studying the carpet.

"I want you to read something first." He went to the other side of the couch and picked up a box that had had been lying on the floor. He carefully handed it to her. "It's the first half of my book."

She smiled with delight. "You're going to let me read it?" She hurriedly lifted the lid and glanced down. There was something highly personal about reading his manuscript.

He started pacing again. "It's a story about two police detectives. I want you to know right now that

Shamus is me. A lot of the stuff he does I did. The way he feels and acts are my feelings."

She tenderly fingered the neatly typed pages. "Are you afraid that this might change how I feel about you?"

"Maybe." He shrugged. "Being a cop isn't an easy job, Erin. Being a good cop is harder still." He jammed his hands into his pockets. "There's another detective in the story. She's a woman and her name is Fiona. I modeled her after you."

"Me?" She laughed. "That really must have taken some imagination."

He looked down at his sneakers. "Hardly any, Erin. It just came naturally." He picked up their dishes. "I'm going to be spending the night over at my place."

She gaped at him. "What? Why?"

"To give you time."

"To read?" She glanced down at the box. There weren't that many pages.

"Yes, but also to think."

"About what?"

"An answer to my question."

"What question was that?" she asked, bewildered.

He headed for the kitchen. "Will you marry me?"

Her mouth dropped open again as he disappeared into the kitchen. A moment later she heard the soft closing of the back door. He was gone.

Erin borrowed one of Bain's traits and paced around the bed. She was starting to get dizzy from traveling the same path over and over again. Bain loved her! She had reread the first half of his book twice and had came to the same conclusion both times. Shamus was in love with Fiona, so that meant Bain was in love with her. He had given Fiona not only some of her sterling qualities but a few of her more questionable ones, too, such as her stubbornness. There weren't any children cluttering up the relationship or, more importantly, holding it together. Shamus loved Fiona for the woman that she was. Didn't that mean Bain loved her, children or not?

Erin asked herself one very important question—did the fact that Bain was Caitlin and Arlene's biological father make that big of a difference to the way she felt toward him? The answer was a definite no. He was the same man who would make a wonderful father for the girls and their unborn child. He was the same man who could make her knees go weak with just a smile and her stomach dip and flutter with the lightest kiss. He was the same man who paced outside the bathroom door every morning while she lost her breakfast, and he was the same man who had hooked up his stereo in the greenhouse so that her ailing plants could listen to classic rock 'n' roll. He was the same man she had fallen in love with.

She smiled as she looked around her room. Traces of Bain were everywhere. His running shorts were thrown over the back of the chair, two of his books were lying on the nightstand, and even the pillow next to hers held the faint scent of his aftershave. Bain belonged in her life and in her bed.

She glanced down at the nightstand where the manuscript lay. She wasn't sure how he was going to end the book, but she had a pretty good idea of how her and Bain's story was going to end: with a happily-ever-after.

She turned off the lights and climbed into bed. Caitlin and Arlene were going to be so excited about getting a real daddy, they probably wouldn't sleep for a week. Junior was using her bladder for a water bed, and her visits to the bathroom had become hourly. Soon the cravings would start. Pickles, ice cream, and pizza were the traditional ones. When *she* craved something, it was usually along the lines of fresh blueberries in December, lemon meringue pie at three in the morning, and anchovies, hold the pizza. She chuckled softly as she hugged his pillow to her breast. Bain deserved everything he had coming to him for making her wait so long.

Bain glanced out the kitchen window one last time before picking up the tray and heading upstairs. Caitlin and Arlene were busy helping Chris spread a layer of gravel in the newly fixed greenhouse. He had slipped Chris an extra ten dollars to keep an eye on the girls till he came for them. Erin and he had a lot to talk about this morning.

He tapped lightly on her closed bedroom door, waited a few seconds, then pushed it open with his hip. Her breakfast dishes rattled softly on the tray. He looked over at Erin and smiled. Her hair was twisted and tangled, and her nightgown was slipping off one creamy shoulder. She looked sexy, seductive, and sweet. "Good morning, sleepyhead." He set the tray down on the nightstand.

Erin rubbed her eyes and yawned. "What time is it?"

"After nine."

"Where are the girls?"

"They're helping Chris spread some gravel in Number Four." He handed her a cup of weak herbal tea and smiled.

She sniffed the tea and took a tentative sip. "More likely they're doing more harm than good."

"Chris enjoys their company, and they enjoy his." He sat and anxiously tapped his fingers on the arm of the chair. His manuscript sat in its box next to her bed, and Erin seemed to be in an awfully good mood that morning. Was that a good sign? The tempo of his tapping increased as she reached for the plate of crackers. When she started to rearrange the unsalted crackers, his control snapped.

"So what do you think?" he asked as calmly as he could.

She took another sip of tea. "You made it a little stronger than usual this morning?"

"Not the tea," he growled. He had spent the entire sleepless night worrying about their future, and all she could comment on was that the tea tasted stronger.

She blinked innocently and glanced at the tray. Tea and crackers was the same breakfast he had been bringing her for the past two weeks. "Are they different crackers?" she asked sweetly, too sweetly.

His fingers stopped tapping and his gaze narrowed. "You're playing with me, aren't you?"

She fluttered her eyelashes in mock innocence. "I can assure you, sir, that my hands haven't touched you."

Bain relaxed. Everything was going to work out. "I can assure you, madame, if they had, you wouldn't be alone in that bed."

She nodded. "Point noted," she said, and took another sip of tea.

He drew in a deep breath. "I knew I loved you for a long time, Erin."

"Because I'm Caitlin and Arlene's mother?"

"No, in spite of it. When I first decided to stay here, I must have told myself a thousand times not to get involved with you. Any kind of relationship with you would just complicate matters."

"And did it?"

"Unmercifully." He became very serious. "I had a hell of a time separating the mother in you from the woman."

"Why didn't you say something to me?"

"At first I didn't want you to think I only wanted you because of Caitlin and Arlene."

She nodded in understanding. "And then I became pregnant."

"Bingo! You were so busy tossing your cookies in the bathroom or passing out that a marriage proposal didn't strike me as too romantic. Sensible, yes, romantic no."

She finished the tea and set the empty cup on the tray. "So when were you going to ask me? Before, after, or perhaps during Junior's birth? That would be one hell of a scene in the delivery room."

"No, I was waiting until you were allowed out of bed."

She fluffed a pillow and placed it behind her back. "I stole your thunder, didn't I?"

"Along with my lightning." He chuckled and knelt on one knee. "I guess I deserve this for keeping you waiting so long." He took her hand and kissed her fingers. "Will you do me the honor of becoming my wife?"

Her expression became one of bewilderment. "I don't know."

"What do you mean 'I don't know'?" he shouted as he jumped to his feet.

"This is a major decision, Bain. I haven't even had time to eat a decent breakfast yet. How do you expect me to make a major decision that will affect the rest of my life on an empty stomach?"

Bain started to pace. "Yesterday you asked me to marry you!"

"That was yesterday, and my stomach was full then." She crossed her arms and pouted. "How do you expect me to make up my mind with all the noise my stomach is making? Flip a coin?"

He stopped in mid-stride and stared at her. The little minx was still playing. "Would you really flip a coin to determine if we get married or not?" He lightly jingled the coins in his pocket.

She eyed him suspiciously and nodded.

He grinned as he pulled a coin from his pocket. "Tails we get married."

She shook her head. "That's your two-sided coin." She reached over to the nightstand where a small pile of coins lay and picked one up. "I say heads we get married."

He stared in horror at the silver coin in her hand. She couldn't be serious. No one flipped quarters over their future. His tongue became untangled when he saw she was ready to toss it. "Erin, wait!"

The coin flew up into the air. "Too late, Bain."

He watched the coin fall, as if in slow motion, into the palm of Erin's hand. He pictured his entire life passing before his eyes as she slapped the coin onto the back of her other hand. His heart left his chest and lodged in his throat as she removed her hand. George Washington's profile was reflected in the early-morning sunlight streaming in through the windows.

She looked at the coin and then up at him. "I guess that means we're getting married."

He dropped down onto the bed and pulled her into his arms. His kisses were hot and swift as he tried to cover every square inch of her face with them. "Don't ever do that to me again." His lips brushed her eyelashes. "I aged ten years with the toss of that coin." Feather-soft kisses covered her jaw. He pulled back and stared at the woman he loved. "Do you really want to get married? You're not just doing it because of the kids or a silly coin toss?"

She held up the coin and grinned. The love she

felt for him was written across her face. "I love you, Bain O'Neil." She handed him the coin.

"I love you, Erin Flynn, soon to be O'Neil." He started to lay the coin back on the table, but Erin's hand stopped him. He followed her glance to the coin. Curiously he opened his palm. George Washington was still in profile. He was beginning to love that president, wooden teeth and all.

Confused by Erin's expression of laughter, he turned the coin over. The profile of George Washington was still staring up at him. The little minx had cheated. "Erin," he growled threateningly.

She chuckled and ran a hand up his thigh. It had only been two weeks, but it felt like forever. "How long did you say the girls will be helping Chris?"

His breath grew uneven as her searching hand traveled higher. "Chris will keep them busy until I come back for them."

Her hand found what it had been searching for, and she smiled as he sucked in his breath. "Good. Now, would you like to flip the coin to see who gets to be on top?"

EPILOGUE

"Mr. O'Neil, you have to hand me the baby now so that I can weigh him." The kindly nurse stood next to him and held out her arms.

Bain tightened his grip on the precious bundle. He had a son! Bain Grady O'Neil, Jr., had made his appearance into the world three minutes ago. He looked down at the baby nestled in a soft hospital blanket and encountered his son's unblinking stare. Bain junior had arrived three weeks early and in record time. The nurse had informed him that Erin's four hours of labor was an excellent time. Still, he had never lived through four hours of such gut-wrenching pain, screaming, and hypertension bordering on cardiac arrest. That was all from him. Erin had pulled through with flying colors.

"Hey, new daddy," she whispered. "The nurse

needs to take him now. It will only be for a minute. She'll bring him right back."

Bain cradled the bundle and ever so lightly brushed his finger across his son's cheek. "He's beautiful, Erin." He gazed at his wife still lying in the birthing bed, being attended to. Tears filled his eyes. "Thank you."

She lifted her hand and brushed at the dark, wet curls covering her son's head. "He's perfect."

The nurse sighed and carefully took the bundle out of his father's arms.

"Be careful," Bain said.

The nurse glanced at Erin. Both of them smiled knowingly. "Don't worry, Mr. O'Neil, I haven't dropped one yet."

Bain stared horrified at the nurse, and Erin chuckled. When he started to rise, Erin said, "Bain, she was only kidding."

He watched the nurse walk over to a scale. Only when he was satisfied that she seemed to know what she was doing did he return his attention to Erin. "Did I tell you how much I loved you today?"

"Only today, huh?" She winced, and Bain glared down at Dr. Priceman, who was still busily working on stuff Bain would rather not know about.

"Easy, Doc," he said.

Dr. Priceman glanced up and smiled. "Sorry."

"Bain," Erin said. "I know we've been joking

about calling him Junior for the past nine months, but I really don't want to call him that for the rest of his life. Forty-year-old Juniors just don't inspire confidence, if you know what I mean." She winced again.

Bain shot a murderous glare back down to the foot of the bed. "Having two Bains in the house could become mighty confusing."

"I was thinking about calling him Grady. After all, it's his middle name."

"Grady?" He looked across the room at his wailing son. Miniature arms and legs were flailing in all different directions. The nurse was putting silver nitrate in his eyes. "I don't know."

"How about if I flip you for it?"

Bain looked down at his wife and brushed a damp curl away from her face. Lord, she was beautiful. He kissed her lightly. So fragile-looking, yet so strong. He pulled a coin from his pocket and playfully tossed it into the air. "Tails it's Grady and heads it's Junior."

Dr. Priceman and the two nurses who were in the room all looked up to follow the flashing coin through the air.

Erin smiled radiantly as the coin landed in the palm of Bain's hand. With a twinkle in his eye he slapped it onto the back of his other hand and uncovered the coin. "Tails it is. I guess it's Grady after all."

The nurse cradling their son looked down and bundled him more tightly into the blanket. "Well, Mr. Grady O'Neil," she said to him, "that's the first time in all my twenty years working here that I ever saw a baby get named by a toss of a coin."

THE EDITOR'S CORNER

It's summertime, and nothing makes the living as easy—and exciting—as knowing that next month six terrific LOVESWEPTs are coming your way. Whether you decide to take them to the beach or your backyard hammock, these novels, written by your favorite authors, are guaranteed to give you hours of sheer pleasure.

Lynne Bryant leads the line-up with **BELIEVING HEART**, LOVESWEPT #630—and one tall, dark, and dangerously handsome hero. Duke King is head of his family's oil company, a man nobody dares to cross, so the last thing he expects is to be shanghaied by a woman! Though Marnie MacBride knows it's reckless to rescue this mogul from a kidnapping attempt single-handedly, she has no choice but to save him. When she sails off with him in her boat, she fancies herself his protector; little does she know that under the magic of a moonlit sky, serious, responsible Duke will throw caution to the wind and, like a swashbuckling pirate, lay claim to the potent pleasures of her lips. Marnie makes Duke think of a seductive sea witch, a feisty Venus, and he's captivated by the sweet magic of her spirit. He wishes he could give her a happy ending to their adventure together, but he knows he can never be what she wants most. And Marnie finds she has to risk all to heal his secret pain, to teach his heart to believe in dreams once more. Lynne has written a beautiful, shimmering love story.

With **ALL FOR QUINN**, LOVESWEPT #631, Kay Hooper ends her *Men of Mysteries Past* series on an unforgettable note—and a truly memorable hero. You've seen Quinn in action in the previous three books of the series, and if you're like any red-blooded woman, you've already lost your heart to this green-eyed prince of thieves. Morgan West certainly has, and that lands her in a bit of a pickle, since Quinn's expected to rob the Mysteries Past exhibit of priceless jewelry at the museum she runs. But how could she help falling under his sensual spell? Quinn's an international outlaw with charm, wit, and intelligence who, in the nine and a half weeks since they have met, has stolen a necklace right off her neck, given her the mocking gift of a concubine ring, then turned up on her doorstep wounded and vulnerable, trusting her with his life. Even as she's being enticed beyond reason, Quinn is chancing a perilous plan that can cost him her love. Pick up a copy and treat yourself to Kay at her absolute best!

Ruth Owen made quite a splash when Einstein, the jive-talking, TV-shopping computer from her first LOVESWEPT, **MELTDOWN,** won a special WISH (Women in Search of a Hero) award from *Romantic Times*. Well, in **SMOOTH OPERATOR,** LOVESWEPT #632, Einstein is back, and this time he has a sister computer with a problem. PINK loves to gamble, you see, and this keeps Katrina Sheffield on her toes. She's in charge of these two super-intelligent machines, and as much as the independent beauty hates to admit it, she needs help containing PINK's vice. Only one person is good enough to involve in this situation—Jack Fagen, the security whiz they call the Terminator. He's a ruthless troubleshooter, the kind of man every mother warns her daughter about, and though Kat should know better, she can't deny that his heat brands her with wildfire. When it becomes obvious that someone is trying to destroy all she's worked for, she has no choice but to rely on Jack to prove her innocence. Superbly combining humor and sensuality, Ruth delivers a must-read.

STORMY WEATHER, LOVESWEPT #633, by Gail Douglas, is an apt description for the turbulent state Mitch Canfield finds himself in from the moment Tiffany Greer enters his life. Though she isn't wearing a sarong and lei when he first catches sight of her, he knows instantly who the pretty woman is. The native Hawaiian has come to Winnipeg in the winter to check out his family's farm for her company, but she's got all the wrong clothes and no idea how cold it can be. Though he doubts she'll last long in the chilly north, he can't help feeling possessive or imagining what it would be like to cuddle with her beside a raging fire—and ignite a few of his own. It seems he's spending half his time making serious promises to himself to keep his hands off her, and the other half breaking those promises. Tiffany wants to keep her mind on business, but she's soon distracted by the cool beauty of the land around her and exhilarated by Mitch's potent kisses. Then she runs into the impenetrable barrier of his mysterious hurt, and she knows she's facing the biggest challenge of her life—to convince Mitch that his arms are the only place she'll ever feel warm again. Gail's luminous writing is simply irresistible.

If intensity is what you've come to expect from a novel by Laura Taylor, then **HEARTBREAKER,** LOVESWEPT #634, will undoubtedly satisfy you. After an explosion renders Naval Intelligence officer Micah Holbrook sightless, he turns furious, hostile, desperate to seize control of his life—and also more magnificently handsome than ever, Bliss Rowland decides. Ever since he saved her life years ago, she's compared every other man she's ever met to him, and no one has measured up. Now that he's come to the island of St. Thomas to begin his recuperation under her care, the last thing she intends to allow is for him to surrender to his fear. It's hard fighting for a man who doesn't want to fight to get better, and the storm of emotions that engulfs them both threatens to destroy her soul. Unsure of his recovery, Micah keeps pushing her away, determined to ignore his hunger to caress her silken skin and the taste of longing on her lips. Knowing that only her passion can heal his pain, Bliss dares him to be conquered by his need. Laura will touch your heart with this stunning love story.

Last, but certainly not least, in the line-up is **CON MAN** by Maris Soule, LOVESWEPT #635. As head of a foundation that provides money for worthy causes, Kurt Jones is definitely no con man, but he knows that's how Micki Bradford will think of him once she learns of his deception. It all starts when, instead of letting his usual investigator check out a prospective grant recipient, he decides he'll try undercover work himself. He arranges a meeting with expert rider Micki, then on the pretense that he's interested in finding a stable for a horse, pumps her for information . . . even as his gaze caresses her and he longs to touch her as she's never been touched. He's tempted to tell her the truth, to promise he'll never hurt her, but Micki has learned the hard way how irresistible a good-looking liar can be. As Kurt sweeps her into a steamy charade to unearth the facts, Kurt vows he'd dare any danger to win Micki's trust, and teach her to have faith in his love. Maris does nothing less than thrill you with this exciting romance.

On sale this month from Bantam are two thrilling novels of passion and intrigue. First is **LADY VALIANT** by the magnificent Suzanne Robinson, whom *Romantic Times* has described as "an author with star quality." In this mesmerizing tale of grand romantic adventure, Thea Hunt is determined to repay the kindness of Mary, Queen of Scots, by journeying to Scotland to warn her away from a treacherous marriage. But in the thick of an English forest, she suddenly finds herself set upon by thieves . . . and chased down by a golden-haired highwayman who stills her struggles—and stirs her heart— with one penetrating glance from his fiery blue eyes. As a spy in Queen Elizabeth's service, Robin St. John is prepared to despise Thea, whom he considers a traitorous wench, to enjoy her torment as he spirits her away to a castle where she'll remain until Mary Stuart is safely wed. But he finds himself desiring her more than any other woman he's ever met. As captive and captor clash, Robin vows to use his every weapon to make Thea surrender to the raging fires of his need and the rising heat of her own passion.

Lois Wolfe returns with **MASK OF NIGHT**, a tantalizing historical romance where one bewitching actress finds love and danger waiting in the wings. Katie Henslowe's prayers are answered the night wealthy railroad tycoon Julian Gates becomes her benefactor, hiring her family's ragtag acting troupe for his new theater. But no sooner has her uncertain world begun to settle down than the potent kiss of a maddeningly attractive stranger sends her reeling. Matt Dennigan is arrogant, enigmatic, and broke—reasons enough for Katie to avoid him. And when, for secret motives of his own, the mysterious rancher begins to draw her into his search for evidence again Julian, Katie tries to resist. But in Matt's heated embrace she finds herself giving in to her innermost longings, only to discover that she and Matt are trapped in a treacherous quest for justice. Against all odds they become partners in a dangerous mission that will take them from a teeming city to the wild frontier, testing the limits of their courage and turning their fiercest desires into spellbinding love. . . .

Also on sale this month, in the hardcover edition from Doubleday, is **SATIN AND STEELE** by the ever-popular Fayrene Preston. Long out of print, this is a wonderfully evocative and uniquely contemporary love story. Skye Anderson knows the joy and wonder of love, as well as the pain of its tragic loss. She's carved a new life for herself at Dallas's Hayes Corporation, finding security in a cocoon of hardworking days and lonely nights. Then her company is taken over by the legendary corporate raider James Steele, and once again Skye must face the possibility of losing everything she cares about. When Steele enlists her aid in organizing the new corporation, she's determined to prove herself worthy of the challenge. But as they work together side by side, she can't deny that she feels more than a professional interest in her new boss—and that the feeling is mutual. Soon she'll have to decide whether to let go of her desire for Steele once and for all—or to risk everything for a second chance at love.

Happy reading!

With warmest wishes,

Nita Taublib

Nita Taublib

Associate Publisher

Don't miss these exciting books by your
favorite Bantam authors

On sale in June:
LADY VALIANT
by *Suzanne Robinson*

MASK OF NIGHT
by *Lois Wolfe*

And in hardcover from Doubleday
SATIN AND STEELE
by *Fayrene Preston*

From the bestselling author of
Lady Defiant, *Lady Hellfire*, and
Lady Gallant . . .

Suzanne Robinson

"An author with star
quality . . . spectacularly talented."
—*Romantic Times*

Lady Valiant

*Breathtakingly talented author Suzanne Robinson spins a
richly romantic new historical romance set during the spellbinding Elizabethan era. LADY VALIANT is the passion-
ate love story of Rob Savage—highwayman, nobleman, and
master spy—and the fiery young beauty he kidnaps.*

A tantalizing glimpse follows . . .

Thea Hunt refused to ride in the coach. Heavy, cumbersome,
and slow, it jounced her so that she nearly vomited after a few
minutes inside it. She preferred riding at the head of her party,
just behind the outriders, in spite of Nan Hobby's objections.
Hobby rode in the coach and shouted at her charge whenever
she felt Thea was riding too fast.

"Miiiiiistress!"

Thea groaned and turned her mare. There was no use trying to ignore Hobby. It only made her shout louder. As the outriders entered the next valley, Thea pulled alongside the coach. The vehicle jolted over a log, causing Hobby to disappear in a flurry of skirts and petticoats.

"Aaaoow," groaned Hobby. "Mistress, my bones, my bones."

"You could ride."

"That horrible mare you gave me can't be trusted."

"Not when you shriek at her and scare her into bolting."

"Aaaaow."

Thea pointed down the track that led into the oak-and-hazel-wooded valley. "We'll be following this road. No more spiny hills for a while."

She glanced up at the hills on either side of the valley. Steeply pitched like tent tops they posed a hazard to the wagons, loaded with chests and furniture, and to the coach. Yet she was glad to see them, for their presence meant northern England. Soon they would reach the border and Scotland. She heard the call of a lapwing in the distance and spotted a merlin overhead. The countryside seemed deserted except for their small party.

She'd insisted on taking as few servants and men-at-arms as necessary in order to travel quickly. She and Hobby were the only women and the men-at-arms numbered only seven including her steward. Still, the baggage and Hobby slowed them down, and she had need of haste.

The Queen of Scots was to marry that fool Darnley. When Grandmother told her the news, at first she hadn't believed it. Clever, beautiful, and softhearted, Her Majesty deserved better than that selfish toad. Thea had pondered long upon Grandmother's suggestion that she go to Scotland. Grandmother said Mary Stuart would listen to no criticism of Darnley, but that she might listen to Thea. After all, they had both shared quarters and tutors with the French royal children.

Thea had been honored with Mary's friendship, for both found themselves foreigners among a clutch of French children. Later, when Thea had need of much more than friendship, Mary had given her aid, had seen to it that Thea was allowed to go home.

Slapping her riding crop on her leg, Thea muttered to herself. "Don't think of it. That time is over. You'll go to Scotland for a time and then return to the country where no one can hurt you."

Nudging her mare, she resumed her place near the front of the line of horses and wagons. Only a cause of great moment could have forced her to leave her seclusion. She'd made her own life far away from any young noblemen. Some called her a hermit. Some accused her of false pride. None suspected the mortal wound she nursed in secret—a wound so grievous and humiliating it had sent her flying from the French court determined to quit the society of the highborn forever.

Her steward interrupted her thoughts. "Mistress, it's close to midday. Shall I look for a place to stop?"

She nodded and the man trotted ahead. Hunger had crept up on her unnoticed, and she tugged at the collar of her riding gown. Her finger caught the edge of one of the gold buttons that ran down the garment, and she felt a sting. Grimacing, she looked at her forefinger. Blood beaded up in a small cut on the side. She sucked the wound and vowed to demand that Hobby remove the buttons. They'd been a gift from Grandmother, but one of them had a sharp edge that needed filing.

It was a good excuse to replace them with the old, plainer buttons she preferred. These were too ornate for her taste. She always felt she should be wearing brocade or velvet with them, and a riding hat, which she detested. Only this morning Hobby had tried to convince her to wear one of those silly jeweled and feathered contrivances on her head. Refusing, she'd stuffed her thick black hair into a net that kept the straight locks out of her way.

She examined her finger. It had stopped bleeding. Pulling her gloves from her belt, she drew them on and searched the path ahead for signs of the steward's return. As she looked past the first outrider, something dropped on the man from the overhanging branches like an enormous fruit with appendages. The second outrider dropped under the weight of another missile and at the same time she heard shouts and grunts from the man behind her.

"Aaaaow! Murder, murder!"

A giant attacked the coach, lumbering over to it and thrusting his arms inside. A scrawny man in a patched cloak toppled into her path as she turned her horse toward the coach. He sprang erect and pointed at her.

"Here, Robin!"

She looked in the direction of the man's gaze and saw a black stallion wheel, his great bulk easily controlled by a golden-haired man who seemed a part of the animal. The stallion and his rider jumped into motion, hooves tearing the earth, the man's long body aligning itself over the horse's neck. Stilled by fright, she watched him control the animal with a strength that seemed to rival that of the stallion.

The brief stillness vanished as she understood that the man who was more stallion than human was coming for her. Fear lanced through her. She kicked her mare hard and sprang away, racing down the path through the trees. Riding sidesaddle, she had a precarious perch, but she tapped her mare with the crop, knowing that the risk of capture by a highwayman outweighed the risk of a fall. Her heart pounding with the hoofbeats of her mare, she fled.

The path twisted to the right and she nearly lost her seat as she rounded the turn. Righting herself, she felt the mare stretch her legs out and saw that the way had straightened. She leaned over her horse, not daring to look behind and lose her balance. Thus she only heard the thunder of hooves and felt the spray of dirt as the stallion caught up. The animal's black head appeared, and she kicked her mare in desperation.

A gloved hand appeared, then a golden head. An arm snaked out and encircled her waist. Thea sailed out of the saddle and landed in front of the highwayman. Terror gave her strength. She wriggled and pounded the imprisoning arm.

"None of that, beastly papist gentry mort."

Understanding little of this, caring not at all, Thea wriggled harder and managed to twist so that she could bite the highwayman's arm. She was rewarded with a howl. Twisting again, she bit the hand that snatched at her hair and thrust herself out of the saddle as the stallion was slowing to a trot.

She landed on her side, rolled, and scrambled to her feet. Ahead she could see her mare walking down the trail in search of grass. Sprinting for the animal, she felt her hair come loose from its net and sail out behind her. Only a few yards and she might escape on the mare.

Too late she heard the stallion. She glanced over her shoulder to see a scowling face. She gave a little yelp as a long, lean body sailed at her. She turned to leap out of range, but the highwayman landed on her. The force of his weight jolted the air from her lungs and she fell. The ground jumped at her face. Her head banged against something. There was a moment of sharp pain and the feeling of smothering before she lost her senses altogether.

Her next thought wasn't quite a thought, for in truth there was room in her mind for little more than feeling. Her head ached. She was queasy and she couldn't summon the strength to open her eyes. She could feel her face because someone had laid a palm against her cheek. She could feel her hand, because someone was holding it.

"Wake you, my prize. I've no winding sheet to wrap you in if you die."

The words were harsh. It was the voice of thievery and rampage, the voice of a masterless man, a highwayman. Her eyes flew open at the thought and met the sun. No, not the sun, bright light filtered through a mane of long, roughly cut tresses. She shifted her gaze to the man's face and saw his lips curve into a smile of combined satisfaction and derision. She could only lie on the ground and blink at him, waiting.

He leaned toward her and she shrank away. Glaring at her, he held her so that she couldn't retreat. He came close, and she was about to scream when he touched the neck of her gown. The feel of his gloved hand on her throat took her voice from her. She began to shake. An evil smile appeared upon his lips, then she felt a tightening of her collar and a rip. She found her voice and screamed as he tore the top button from her gown. Flailing at him weakly, she drew breath to scream again, but he clamped a hand over her mouth.

"Do you want me to stuff my gloves into your mouth?"

She stared at him, trapped by his grip and the malice in his dark blue eyes.

"Do you?"

She shook her head.

"Then keep quiet."

He removed his hand and she squeezed her eyes shut, expecting him to resume his attack. When nothing happened, she peeped at him from beneath her lashes. He was regarding her with a contemptuous look, but soon transferred his gaze to the button in his palm. He pressed it between his fingers, frowned at it, then shoved it into a pouch at his belt.

"I'll have the rest of them later," he said.

Reaching for her, he stopped when she shrank from him. He hesitated, then grinned at her.

"Sit you up by yourself then."

Still waiting for him to pounce on her, she moved her arms, but when she tried to shove herself erect, she found them useless. He snorted. Gathering her in his arms, he raised her to a sitting position. She winced at the pain in her head. His hand came up to cradle her cheek and she moaned.

"If you puke on me I'll tie you face down on your horse for the ride home."

Fear gave way to anger. In spite of her pain, she shoved at his chest. To her chagrin, what she thought were mortal blows turned out to be taps.

"Aaaow! Look what you've done to my lady."

"Get you gone, you old cow. She's well and will remain so, for now. Stubb, put the maid on a horse and let's fly. No sense waiting here for company any longer."

Thea opened her eyes. The highwayman was issuing orders to his ruffians. From her position she could see the day's growth of beard on his chin and the tense cords of muscle in his neck.

"My—my men."

"Will have a long walk," he snapped.

"Leave us," she whispered, trying to sit up. "You have your booty."

The highwayman moved abruptly to kneel in front of her. Taking her by the shoulders, he pulled her so that they faced each other eye to eye.

"But Mistress Hunt, you are the booty. All the rest is fortune's addition."

"But—"

He ignored her. Standing quickly, he picked her up. Made dizzy by the sudden change, she allowed her head to drop to his shoulder. She could smell the leather of his jerkin and feel the soft cambric of his shirt. An outlaw who wore cambric shirts.

She was transferred to the arms of another ruffian, a wiry man no taller than she with a crooked nose and a belligerent expression. Her captor mounted the black stallion again and reached down.

"Give her to me."

Lifted in front of the highwayman, she was settled in his lap a great distance from the ground. The stallion danced sideways and his master put a steadying hand on the animal's neck. The stallion calmed at once.

"Now, Mistress Hunt, shall I tie your hands, or will you behave? I got no patience for foolish gentry morts who don't know better than to try outrunning horses."

Anger got the better of her. "You may be sure the next time I leave I'll take your horse."

"God's blood, woman. You take him, and I'll give you the whipping you've asked for."

His hand touched a whip tied to his saddle and she believed him. She screamed and began to struggle.

"Cease your nattering, woman."

He fastened his hand over her mouth again. His free arm wrapped around her waist. Squeezing her against his hard body, he stifled her cries. When she went limp from lack of air, he released her.

"Any more yowling and I'll gag you."

Grabbing her by the shoulders, he drew her close so that she was forced to look into his eyes. Transfixed by their scornful beauty, she remained silent.

"What say you?" he asked. "Shall I finish what I began and take all your buttons?"

Hardly able to draw breath, she hadn't the strength to move her lips.

"Answer, woman. Will you ride quietly, or fight beneath me on the ground again?"

"R—ride."

Chuckling he turned her around so that her back was to his chest and called to his men. The outlaw called Stubb rode up leading a horse carrying Hobby, and Thea twisted her head around to see if her maid fared well.

"Look here, Rob Savage," Stubb said. "If you want to scrap with the gentry mort all day, I'm going on. No telling when someone else is going to come along, and I'm not keen on another fight this day."

"Give me a strap then."

A strap. He was going to beat her. Thea gasped and rammed her elbow into Rob's stomach. She writhed and twisted, trying to escape the first blow from the lash. Rob finally trapped her by fastening his arms about her and holding her arms to her body.

"Quick, Stubb, tie her hands with the strap."

Subsiding, Thea bit her lower lip. Her struggles had been for naught. Rob's arm left her, but he shook her by the shoulders.

"Now be quiet or I'll tie you to a pack horse."

"Aaaow! Savage, Robin Savage, the highwayman. God preserve us. We're lost, lost. Oh, mistress, it's Robin Savage. He's killed hundreds of innocent souls. He kills babes and ravages their mothers and steals food from children and burns churches and dismembers clergymen and—"

Thea felt her body grow cold and heavy at the same time. She turned and glanced up at the man who held her. He was frowning at the hysterical Hobby. Suddenly he looked down at her. One of his brows lifted and he smiled slowly.

"A body's got to have a calling."

"You—you've done these things?"

"Now how's a man to remember every little trespass and sin, especially a man as busy as me?"

He grinned at her, lifted a hand to his men, and kicked the stallion. Her head was thrown back against his chest. He steadied her with an arm around her waist, but she squirmed away from him. He ignored her efforts and pulled her close as the horse sprang into a gallop. She grasped his arm with her bound hands, trying to pry it loose to no avail. It was as much use for a snail to attempt to move a boulder.

The stallion leaped over a fallen sapling and she clutched at Savage's arm. Riding a small mare was a far less alarming experience than trying to keep her seat on this black giant. She would have to wait for a chance to escape, but escape she must.

This man was a villain with a price on his head. She remembered hearing of him now. He and his band roamed the highways of England doing murder and thievery at will. Savage would appear, relieve an honest nobleman or merchant of his wealth and vanish. No sheriff or constable could find him.

As they rode, Thea mastered her fears enough to begin to think. This man wanted more than just riches and rape. If he'd only wanted these things, he could have finished his attack when he'd begun it. And it wasn't as if she were tempting to men, a beauty worth keeping. She'd found that out long ago in France. And this Savage knew her name. The mystery calmed her somewhat. Again she twisted, daring a glance at him.

"Why have you abducted me?"

He gaped at her for a moment before returning his gaze to the road ahead. "For the same reason I take any woman. For using."

He slowed the stallion and turned off the road. Plunging into the forest, they left behind the men assigned to bring the coach and wagons. Several thieves went ahead, while Stubb and the rest followed their master. Thea summoned her courage to break the silence once more.

"Why else?"

"What?"

"It can't be the only reason, to, to . . ."

"Why not?"

"You know my name. You were looking for me, not for just anyone."

"Is that so?"

"Are you going to hold me for ransom? There are far richer prizes than me."

"Ransom. Now there's a right marvelous idea. Holding a woman for ransom's a pleasureful occupation."

As he leered down at her, fear returned. Her body shook. She swallowed and spoke faintly.

"No."

There was a sharp gasp of exasperation from Savage. "Don't you be telling me what I want."

"But you can't."

His gaze ran over her face and hair. The sight appeared to anger him, for he cursed and snarled at her.

"Don't you be telling me what I can do. God's blood, woman, I could throw you down and mount you right here."

She caught her lower lip between her teeth, frozen into her own horror by his threats. He snarled at her again and turned her away from him, holding her shoulders so that she couldn't face him. Though he used only the strength of his hands, it was enough to control her, which frightened her even more.

"I could do it," he said. "I might if you don't keep quiet. Mayhap being mounted a few times would shut you up."

Thea remained silent, not daring to anger him further. She had no experience of villains. This one had hurt her. He might hurt her worse. She must take him at his word, despite her suspicion that he'd planned to hold her for ransom. She must escape. She must escape with Hobby and find her men.

They rode for several hours through fells and dales, always heading south, deeper into England. She pondered hard upon how to escape as they traveled. Freeing herself from Savage was impossible. He was too strong and wary of her after her first attempt. She might request a stop to relieve herself, but the foul man might insist upon watching her. No, she would have to wait until they stopped for the night and hope he didn't tie her down.

Her gorge rose at the thought of what he might do once they stopped. She tried to stop her body from trembling, but failed. Her own helplessness frightened her and she struggled not to let tears fall. If she didn't escape, she would fight. It seemed to be her way, to keep fighting no matter how useless the struggle.

As dusk fell they crossed a meadow and climbed a rounded hill. At the top she had a view of the countryside. Before her stretched a great forest, its trees so thick she could see nothing but an ocean of leaves.

Savage led his men down the hillside and into the forest. As they entered, the sun faded into a twilight caused by the canopy of leaves about them. Savage rode on until the twilight had almost vanished. Halting in a clearing by a noisy stream, he lifted Thea down.

She'd been on the horse so long and the hours of fear had wearied her so much that her legs buckled under her. Savage caught her, his hands coming up under her arms, and she stumbled against him. Clutching her, he swore. She looked up at him to find him glaring at her again. She caught her breath, certain he would leap upon her.

His arms tightened about her, but he didn't throw her to the ground. Instead, he stared at her. Too confused at the moment to be afraid, she stared back. Long moments passed while they gazed at each other, studying, wary, untrusting.

When he too seemed caught in a web of reverie her fears gradually eased. Eyes of gentian blue met hers and she felt a stab of pain. To her surprise, looking at him had caused the pain. Until that moment she hadn't realized a man's mere appearance could delight to the point of pain.

It was her first long look at him free of terror. Not in all her years in the fabulous court of France had she seen such a man. Even his shoulders were muscled. They were wide in contrast to his hips and he was taller than any Frenchman. He topped any of his thievish minions and yet seemed unaware of the effect of his appearance. Despite his angelic coloring, however, he had the disposition of an adder. He was scowling at her, as if something had caught him unprepared and thus annoyed him. Wariness and fear rushed to the fore again.

"Golden eyes and jet black hair. Why did you have to be so—God's blood, woman." He thrust her away from him. "Never you mind. You were right anyway, little papist. I'm after ransom."

Bewildered, she remained where she was while he stalked away from her. He turned swiftly to point at her.

"Don't you think of running. If I have to chase you and

wrestle with you again, you'll pay in any way I find amusing."
He marched off to shout ill-tempered orders at his men.

Hobby trotted up to her and began untying the leather strap
that bound her hands. Thea stared at Robin Savage, frightened
once more and eyeing his leather-clad figure. How could she have
forgotten his cruelty and appetite simply because he had a lush,
well-formed body and eyes that could kindle wet leaves? She
watched him disappear into the trees at the edge of the clearing,
and at last she was released from the bondage of his presence.

"He's mad," she said.

"Mad, of course, he's mad," Hobby said. "He's a thief and
a murderer and a ravager."

"How could God create such a man, so—so pleasing to the
eye and so evil of spirit?"

"Take no fantasy about this one, mistress. He's a foul villain
who'd as soon slit your throat as spit on you."

"I know." Thea bent and whispered to Hobby. "Can you
run fast and long? We must fly this night. Who knows what will
happen to us once he's done settling his men."

"I can run."

"Good. I'll watch for my chance and you do as well." She
looked around at the men caring for horses and making a fire.
Stubb watched them as he unloaded saddlebags. "For now, I
must find privacy."

Hobby pointed to a place at the edge of the clearing where
bushes grew thick. They walked toward it unhindered. Hobby
stopped at the edge of the clearing to guard Thea's retreat. Thea
plunged into the trees looking for the thickest bushes. Thrusting a low-hanging branch aside, she rounded an oak tree. A tall
form blocked her way. Before she could react, she was thrust
against the tree, and a man's body pressed against hers.

Robin Savage held her fast, swearing at her. She cast a
frightened glance at him, but he wasn't looking at her. He was
absorbed in studying her lips. His anger had faded and his
expression took on a somnolent turbulence. He leaned close and
whispered in her ear, sending chills down her spine.

"Running away in spite of my warnings, little papist."

Thea felt a leg shove between her thighs. His chest pressed
against her breasts, causing her to pant. He stared into her eyes
and murmured.

"Naughty wench. Now I'll have to punish you."

Mask of Night
by
Lois Wolfe

author of *The Schemers*

A spectacular new historical romance that combines breath-taking intrigue and suspense with breathless passion.

She was an actress who made her living spinning dreams. He was a rancher turned spy whose dreams had all been bitterly broken. Against all odds, they became partners in a danger-ous mission that would take them from the teeming city to the wild frontier, testing the limits of their courage, and turning their fiercest desires into spellbinding love . . .

Read on for a taste of this unforgettable tale.

What use Gates might have for Katie was immediately apparent when Matt saw her emerge from the cloakroom in an understated emerald green gown. He made note of the dress, especially the top of it, the part that wasn't there. Nice swoop.

Real nice swoop.

Other men noticed too, as she crossed the lobby to the front desk. Matt debated following her. He was already late for dinner with the Senator, but, hell, a little more close observation couldn't hurt.

He joined her at the front desk. Her expression showed annoyance the moment she saw him, and he guessed she regret-ted trying to be polite to him.

"Looks like we both have business here," he said, leaning on the counter.

She turned her back on him, leaving him free to study her, the indignant thrust of her shoulders, the fragile trough of her spine. A wisp of dark golden hair had escaped its pin and rested in the curve of her neck.

"I'm here to meet my brother, Edmund Henslowe," she told the desk clerk.

The clerk went off to check the message boxes. She cocked her chin to her shoulder and sent Matt a withering look.

Hazel, he thought. Her eyes were hazel, more green than brown.

"Miss Katie Henslowe?" the clerk asked when he returned. "Mr. Henslowe wishes you to join him in his suite."

She was obviously startled. "His suite? Here?"

"Sixth floor. Number nineteen."

Six nineteen, Matt thought, looking ahead and not at her.

"Thank you." Icy, perfunctory. She was miffed.

The clerk had business at the other end of the long front desk, and they were alone for a moment.

She stood silent awhile, then turned to Matt. "Did you get all that?"

He was cautious. "What?"

"Don't play dumb. It looks too natural on you. Nice piece of news, wasn't it? The fact that my brother has a room here? Makes it seem like he has money, doesn't it? Well, let me assure you, you and whichever of our creditors you're the snoop for, Poppy does *not* have funds to make payments."

Matt played along, glancing around the opulent lobby. "This doesn't exactly look like a place for the destitute."

"I know." She backed down, stiffly. "Just, please, try to understand. My brother is here only to develop resources for the troupe. Now, I'm sure your loan department will be glad to hear that we may have the potential to resume quarterly payments." She paused. "You *are* a bank agent for Philadelphia Savings, aren't you?"

He shook his head.

"New York Fiduciary?"

"No."

"You work in the private sector, then, for an individual?"

"You could say that."

She looked away. "It's about Edmund, isn't it?"

"How'd you guess?"

Her glance took in his unfashionable attire and worn shoes. "My brother tends to attract an eclectic and, sometimes, illicit crowd."

"Which one am I? Eclectic or illicit?"

"You're a coward and a spy, and I doubt that you've got enough grapeshot in the bag to so much as fire off your name."

He looked at her for a long time. "Insults like that don't come from a lady."

"No." She held his gaze. "And they don't apply to a gentleman."

"Look, I'm not one of your brother's Jack Nasty lowlifes."

"You're not? And yet you have business here?" She studied him thoughtfully. "Are you meeting the senator then?"

Christ, how'd she know? He felt himself grow stony-faced, trying to keep reaction to a minimum.

"I remember," she went on, "seeing you waylay the distinguished senator backstage, Mr. . . . . ?" She waited again for his name.

"Nasty," he said curtly. "Jack Nasty."

"I thought so."

To his surprise, she sidled close and put a hand on his arm. "Sir?" she called to the desk clerk. "My friend here has a request."

Matt tensed. What was she doing?

"Yes, sir?" the clerk asked, returning to them.

"He needs his messages," Katie interjected before Matt could speak.

"Of course." The clerk turned to Matt. "What is the name?"

Damn her.

She smiled prettily at him. "Now, come on. Don't dawdle," she said, as to a child. "You'll make us both late."

He hated being manipulated. He especially hated a woman who did it so well.

She patted his hand. "I know you've had a terrible sore throat." She turned to the clerk. "Maybe if you could just lean close, so he can whisper."

The clerk looked dubious, but obligingly leaned over the counter.

Matt felt pressure rise inside him like steam in a boiler.

"Still hurts?" she asked. "Would it be easier if you just spell it? I'm sure—"

"Dennigan!" The word shot out from between gritted teeth.

The clerk stared, astonished.

Katie removed her hand from his. "See how much better you sound when you try?" she said, then turned to the clerk. "Please check the message box for Mr. Dennigan."

Matt leaned close so no one would see him grab her wrist, grab it hard. "Dennigan," he repeated. "Matt Dennigan."

"Charmed, I'm sure."

She jerked her arm free as the clerk returned. His manner was noticeably more unctuous toward Matt. "Mr. Dennigan? It seems Senator Cahill is waiting dinner for you in the Walker Room."

"The Walker Room," Katie said. "Isn't that the salon for very private dining?"

The clerk nodded again. "Yes, ma'am. Right through the arch and turn left."

Katie looked at Matt. "Well, now, Matt, enjoy your dinner."

She was gracious in triumph, almost sweet, he thought, as she left him. She hurried to the elevator foyer. He stood a long while, watching until the accordion gate of the elevator collapsed sideways to let her on.

She had taken his amateurish game of sleuth and, in one polished play, raised the ante to life-or-death for the Senator's investigation. If she dared mention Matt Dennigan and Senator Cahill in the same breath to the cutthroat millionaire he was about to meet, the game was over. Julian Gates would run for cover and retaliate with all the congressional influence—and hired guns—his money could buy.

Jesus Christ.

OFFICIAL RULES

To enter the sweepstakes below carefully follow all instructions found elsewhere in this offer.

The **Winners Classic** will award prizes with the following approximate maximum values: 1 Grand Prize: $26,500 (or $25,000 cash alternate); 1 First Prize: $3,000; 5 Second Prizes: $400 each; 35 Third Prizes: $100 each; 1,000 Fourth Prizes: $7.50 each. Total maximum retail value of Winners Classic Sweepstakes is $42,500. Some presentations of this sweepstakes may contain individual entry numbers corresponding to one or more of the aforementioned prize levels. To determine the Winners, individual entry numbers will first be compared with the winning numbers preselected by computer. For winning numbers not returned, prizes will be awarded in random drawings from among all eligible entries received. Prize choices may be offered at various levels. If a winner chooses an automobile prize, all license and registration fees, taxes, destination charges and, other expenses not offered herein are the responsibility of the winner. If a winner chooses a trip, travel must be complete within one year from the time the prize is awarded. Minors must be accompanied by an adult. Travel companion(s) must also sign release of liability. Trips are subject to space and departure availability. Certain black-out dates may apply.

The following applies to the sweepstakes named above:

No purchase necessary. You can also enter the sweepstakes by sending your name and address to: P.O. Box 508, Gibbstown, N.J. 08027. Mail each entry separately. Sweepstakes begins 6/1/93. Entries must be received by 12/30/94. Not responsible for lost, late, damaged, misdirected, illegible or postage due mail. Mechanically reproduced entries are not eligible. All entries become property of the sponsor and will not be returned.

Prize Selection/Validations: Selection of winners will be conducted no later than 5:00 PM on January 28, 1995, by an independent judging organization whose decisions are final. Random drawings will be held at 1211 Avenue of the Americas, New York, N.Y. 10036. Entrants need not be present to win. Odds of winning are determined by total number of entries received. Circulation of this sweepstakes is estimated not to exceed 200 million. All prizes are guaranteed to be awarded and delivered to winners. Winners will be notified by mail and may be required to complete an affidavit of eligibility and release of liability which must be returned within 14 days of date on notification or alternate winners will be selected in a random drawing. Any prize notification letter or any prize returned to a participating sponsor, Bantam Doubleday Dell Publishing Group, Inc., its participating divisions or subsidiaries, or the independent judging organization as undeliverable will be awarded to an alternate winner. Prizes are not transferable. No substitution for prizes except as offered or as may be necessary due to unavailability, in which case a prize of equal or greater value will be awarded. Prizes will be awarded approximately 90 days after the drawing. All taxes are the sole responsibility of the winners. Entry constitutes permission (except where prohibited by law) to use winners' names, hometowns, and likenesses for publicity purposes without further or other compensation. Prizes won by minors will be awarded in the name of parent or legal guardian.

Participation: Sweepstakes open to residents of the United States and Canada, except for the province of Quebec. Sweepstakes sponsored by Bantam Doubleday Dell Publishing Group, Inc., (BDD), 1540 Broadway, New York, NY 10036. Versions of this sweepstakes with different graphics and prize choices will be offered in conjunction with various solicitations or promotions by different subsidiaries and divisions of BDD. Where applicable, winners will have their choice of any prize offered at level won. Employees of BDD, its divisions, subsidiaries, advertising agencies, independent judging organization, and their immediate family members are not eligible.

Canadian residents, in order to win, must first correctly answer a time limited arithmetical skill testing question. Void in Puerto Rico, Quebec and wherever prohibited or restricted by law. Subject to all federal, state, local and provincial laws and regulations. For a list of major prize winners (available after 1/29/95): send a self-addressed, stamped envelope entirely separate from your entry to: Sweepstakes Winners, P.O. Box 517, Gibbstown, NJ 08027. Requests must be received by 12/30/94. DO NOT SEND ANY OTHER CORRESPONDENCE TO THIS P.O. BOX.